OTHER

Floyd County

Images of America

Cherokee County

History of The Cherokee Nation

I Am Not As My Fathers Were

YOU BE THE JUDGE

To Jason, Jr. My Nephew

▲▲▲▲▲▲

B. G. McElwee, Sr.
B. G. McElwee, Sr.

May life always be kind to you.

Copyright © 2003 by B.G. McElwee
ISBN 0-9745741-8-X

Published by: McElwee Publishing
P.O. Box 465
Cave Spring, GA 30124

Printing by:
Diversified Digital
309 W. Patton
Lafayette, GA 30728
www.divdigital.com

This book is dedicated to
my wife Tere, my sons
Bobby, Gary and Joe.

To the other family members
whose names I used
within the book

and

Doctor Leonard Reeves and
his family whose names
I also used

This books contains condensed versions of three books

SMITH VALLEY ALABAMA

A story derived from true facts.

YOU CAN SURVIVE AMERICA'S FINAL WAR

Is this America's future? Current events seem to indicate that it is.

VIET NAM 1966-67

A true life story of the period of time this author spend in Johnson's Hell

INTRODUCTION TO
SMITH VALLEY ALABAMA

Legends are not created by birth. No man is born to be one. They are formed from individuals with extraordinary accomplishments. These people are talked and written about from one generation to another, until the facts of their lives become greatly distorted. If most legends could hear or read the stories of them written and oral, they would not recognize that they were the subject. Such are the tales of my Great-Grandfather William Anderson (Belltree) Smith. If all that has been written about him were true, Jesse James and Billy the Kid would seem as choirboys by comparison.

From my early youth, I had listened to tales and read articles about Belltree Smith. The older I got the more ridiculous they became. I shrugged off the stories until 1954. In High School we were studying myths and legends. The teacher stated, "There is a well-known legend here in this area." She then proceeded to tell her version of Belltree Smith. I stood up and informed her that she was talking about my Great-Grandfather. Her response was, "Bobby sit down you know that is not true. There was no such man as Belltree Smith. He is only a myth." I vowed to myself, "One day I will learn and write the truth about this man."

As with most people, I became busy with my own life and forgot about my vow. In the 1990's my cousins Edna (Smith) Stephens and Shirley (Smith) Dowdy began researching the life of William Anderson Smith. Several years were spent gathering the information used to write this story.

It turns out, William A. (Belltree) Smith was more like characters portrayed by John Wayne, in western movies, than Billy The Kid. He was a tall handsome man with black hair and blue eyes who bothered no one. However; he never backed down when confronted with a fight.

Stories of Belltree Smith range from, he was a kind and loving man to tales of the bizarre. It is well documented that under normal circumstances he was a thoughtful and giving man. He was a landowner, farmer and businessman who became a legend because of his mannerisms. His property was his domain and he protected it zealously.

These writings carry a reader through the life and tragic untimely death of William A. (Belltree) Smith and the lives of his family. Will was a man who, had he been privileged to a formal education would have been written about more in history books than in made up newspaper articles.

William Anderson (Belltree) Smith

SMITH VALLEY ALABAMA

Belltree Smith mass murderer, desperado, marauder, scoundrel, myth or victim of unusual circumstances beyond his control? As I lay down his life story you the reader are to be the judge.

In each family, there are a variety of personalities. The average person is endowed with both good and evil traits. The circumstances in which one finds themselves can dictate their destiny. All too often those outside the true ring of knowledge base their assessment of an individual on here-say and gossip. It is impossible to properly judge someone without all the facts.

Each person's life is an adventure. Some individuals live almost singularly and effect few while others effect many, both during their life and after their death. William Anderson (Belltree) Smith's life is a story often told and written about even today over ninety-five years after his death. As happens with most that become legends, the truth becomes distorted. The life of Belltree is one of these. The truth in his case is as dramatic as the now told tales of him. Let us travel, by way of these writings, with him through his actual life's story beginning with his heritage.

George Smith and his young wife Fathy had no idea what the future held for them when they moved west from South Carolina. As with many other families, they dreamed of a better life and ownership of their own land. So in 1825, they followed the migration west along the Fall Line Trail in search of their destiny.

When Fathy discovered that she was pregnant and unable to travel on to their original destination Cherokee County,

Alabama. George decided to settle temporarily in Richmond County, Georgia. He built a cabin and farmed to feed his family. Milton Smith was born here July 29, 1825. Fathy was to bear three more children during their time in Georgia.

George vowed to one day continue his quest to settle in Alabama but a logging accident ended his dream. He was buried under the shade, of a large oak tree.

Melton promised on his father's grave to continue the dream of moving the family to Alabama and soon as he thought his siblings were old enough to travel he prepared them for the journey. In 1845, they loaded two wagons with the family's earthly possessions and set course for Alabama.

The Smith family planted their roots in a valley just south of a mountain range. There was ample water as a mountain stream ran down from between the two tallest mountains. Their valley later became known as Smith Valley. Milton climbed the steep face of the tallest mountain placed an American Flag there and named it Flagpole Mountain. Most people in the area still call it that today. The State of Alabama later named the range The Indian Mountains.

It had been seven years since the Cherokee Indians were forced out. The area was a true wilderness. The Cherokee had kept the forest clear of underbrush with a yearly spring burning. Since their forced removal what had been cleared land for homes and gardens, plus the forest had overgrown with brush, small trees and brambles.

The Smith family set about clearing a site for a house. They first built a small two room house where they lived until they could raise the money for a larger house. The entire family worked. The mother and daughters cleared the area where the

Cherokee once had a garden and planted it with corn, squash, beans and other vegetables.

Starting in 1845, riverboats made regular trips on the Coosa river from Rome, Georgia through Alabama to the Gulf of Mexico. The boats picked up and delivered mail and merchandise up and down the river. Milton with his brothers started a lumber business. The boys downed trees, cut them into logs, hauled them to the river and shipped them to market.

Steamboats on the Coosa River docked at Garrett's Ferry to load and unload their cargo. Passengers and locally produced items left Cherokee County destined for far away places; goods from all over the world were delivered to area stores. The *John J. Seay* burned and sank at Cedar Bluff with all cargo lost in 1888. When railroads were built in the area, riverboats were unable to compete with them and slowly faded away.

Milton was very efficient and soon had sufficient funds to start building a larger house. He was determined that his family would live in a fine home. He began to select and cut trees, which were milled into the lumber needed. He ordered windows and doors from mills in South Carolina. Their furniture had consisted mostly of homemade items. So he ordered furniture from various places and restroom fixtures from England.

The Smith family built a beautiful two-storied antebellum home with a bedroom for each member of the family and a railed veranda on each level.

Milton sometimes hauled vegetables grown on the farm to market in Cedartown, Georgia. A town just a few miles east of his home. One day as he walked down the street he saw the most beautiful woman he had ever seen. He stared it awe as she passed him and smiled. A stranger observed this and said to Milton.

"A lot of women is she not."

"Do you know who she is?"

"That's Catherine Elizabeth Peek. Her family is well known here about."

"Where does she live?"

"Well I hear she lives in Etna."

Milton vowed to himself that she would one day be his wife. He made inquires, learned where Elizabeth attended church and began to attend services there. He finely was introduced to Elizabeth by a new found friend and began a courtship that ended in marriage February 10, 1857.

Life was good, for the Smith family, but trouble was brewing, for the nation. Tensions against the northern dominated United States Congress were at a boiling point, in 1860. Laws were being passed which applied only to the south. Northern big business interest and politicians pressed the south to stay a farming only area. Anyone building a factory in the south was required to pay unfair penalties. Products manufactured in the south were subjected to an import tax if shipped north across the Mason Dixon Line. The same did not apply to northern products shipped south. In 1861, Alabama seceded from the United States and along with six other southern states formed The Confederate States of America.

Although the United States Constitution states that this was a legal act. President Abe Lincoln ordered an invasion to bring these runaway states back into the union. When the invasion began the south immediately formed an army of volunteers to defend itself. Over one half million men died and thousands more were wounded in the next four years. Approximately 365,000 from the north and 200,000 from the south paid with their lives during this war.

At age thirty-six, Milton along with his brothers William and Thomas answered their new nations call to arms and voluntarily joined Company H, 5th Regiment, Alabama Calvary, Marchbank Warrens Battalion. Although William and Milton were too old to be drafted, they felt that they must help protect their families and homes against the invaders and joined the army to do so. Before the end of the war men as old as in their seventies joined the army in a futile attempt to hold back the invading Northern horde. Most of the men and women in the Confederate Army were volunteers untrained in warfare. They were however starch defenders of their homeland and thus adapted rapidly to the situation that faced them.

Milton was wounded in the shoulder during the Battles for Atlanta. As the Confederate Army retreated from Georgia into Alabama, his commanding officer spoke to him.

"Sergeant I understand your home is a few miles south of here."

Milton pointed at Flagpole Mountain in the distance. "Yes sir just south of that mountain."

"Go home soldier and recover. You can rejoin us later."

Milton never returned to the Confederate Army as the war was over by the time he was well enough to do so.

Fathy had never seen such a wonderful sight as when she saw the ragged wounded soldier staggering up the path toward her. She yelled to Elizabeth.

"Hurry help me Milton has come home."

Elizabeth ran to meet him and they embraced. As tears ran down her cheeks.

"I prayed each night that God would send you safely home and at last you are here."

Milton with a weak voice.

"I too prayed each night, for God to look after you and the rest of the family."

Elizabeth then noticed. He was wounded.

"Let me and mother help you the rest of the way."

Milton finished his journey home on the arms of the women he loved his wife and his mother. The war was over for this soldier.

Elizabeth cleaned and redressed his wound as Fathy warmed water for a much needed bath. The war ended in 1865. William and Thomas returned home, the following year and the family was once again united. The Smith's were more fortunate than most southern families as only Milton had suffered a physical injury in the war. Emotional scars however lingered for the rest of their lives.

Most of the fighting had been either north or east of their valley, and no Yankee plundering parties had robbed them of their possessions. Thus, the Smith's were able to stow away food and goods that during normal times would have been sent to market. Their livestock and gardens had been expanded awaiting a pending disaster. Elizabeth, Fathy and the children had maintained the farm while Milton and his brothers were away fighting for the south's freedom.

As Sherman's Army pressed deeper into Georgia many families (mostly women and children) fled the fighting and passed the Smith's house looking for a safe haven. Many were so sick or weary they could travel no further. All were ragged and hungry and few knew their destination. Elizabeth rationed out food and the family provided for the travelers as best they could. A make shift hospital was setup in the house to care for those who could no longer care for themselves. The barn and sheds were converted into temporary shelters.

As soon as they were able, most of the travelers continues their journey westward, but several asked to stay and work for the Smith Family. They built cabins and most became sharecroppers on Smith land.

Near the war's end, a family of former slaves came to the Smith's house. The father and mother had fed their six small children most of the food they had foraged along the way. The children were undernourished and the parents were near starvation. They were too weak and sick to continue. Fathy and Elizabeth took them in, fed and cared for them until they recovered. Milton had never owned slaves but there were Negroes in his Confederate Company and he had come to know most of them to be honorable men. Soldiers get to know each other quiet well and very soon find out who is trustworthy and who is not.

When they felt better Elizabeth inquired of them..

" What are your names and where did you come from?"

"I is Jasmen and he's Jim. We belonged to Mr. Dunwood. The Yankees done come and says we is free. They done told us to leave. We hides in thu woods til they is gone. Then we goes back. Mr. Dunwood is dead and Missess Sara is bad off. Them damm Yankees done took everything any of us had. There was no food and nothing to cook it in if we had some. They even took the curtains and bedclothes. We helped Misses Sara as best we could but she just up and died.

Jim buried them in the family graveyard. We didn't know's what to do. Other Negroes passed by and told us their masters had said they couldn't care for them as they had little or nothing for themselves. Some says they had heard things were better in the west. We gathered the scraps the Yankees done left and start walking."

Milton was sadden by their story. During the war, he had heard how the carpetbaggers followed behind the union army and stole the rest of what people had that the army had not already taken. He had prayed many a time that God would protect his family and he now knew his prays were answered.

" Jim, you and your family can live in the cabin we just finished up the hollow and sharecrop the land."

"Thank you sir but we don't know's nothing about farming. We is house servants."

"Most people don't when they first start but you'll learn day by day. If you and your family work at it hard enough in a few years, you will be able to buy some land of your own."

"Well sir we thanks you and w'll do our best to become farmers."

Thus it was agreed that the new Dunwood family would stay and work for the Smith's as sharecroppers. This event brought about a loyalty to the Smith family from most Negroes in the area for many years.

Melton could never have guessed what the future held for his family. He would recover from his wounds, sire eleven children, homestead his own land, form businesses and suffer a violent death. Of his eleven children, none would obtain the success and notoriety of his son William Anderson who became a legend in his own time.

William Anderson was born the fifth child of Milton and Elizabeth Peek Smith July 16, 1869. Children learned early that they were to handle chores and work the fields. By age six Will was feeding the stock, carrying stove wood and doing what else he was told to do. As Will grew he took on more and more task around the farm. It must be noted that children matured much faster then, than in modern times. Life was hard but the family was accustomed to hard work with little reward.

The Smith's purchased more land, cleared it, planted crops on part of it and sharecropped with less fortunate families on the rest. They built charcoal pits and sold the charcoal to the foundries and also sent lumber and farm products to markets down river.

Milton believed in the Golden Rule, "Do Unto Others As You Would Have Them Do Unto You," and taught his children to respect the needs of others. Will learned from his father that helping those in need to help themselves paid good dividends later. Will's father had worked himself out, of poverty, established a business, built a fine home and become financially independent.

The south was still under the repressive yolk of the north during Will's early years. Yankees looking to make a fortune on small investments came to Cherokee County. The area was rich with iron ore. Mines were started and four furnaces were built to smelt the ore into pig iron. The infamous William Tecumseh Sherman and others had a furnace built near the Alabama /Georgia line and named the community which sprang up around it Tecumseh. The outsiders also started other businesses. Local residents were hired as workers and the area slowly recovered from the war.

Some were not so happy as they considered this another Yankee invasion. The newcomers literally formed and ran a new governing body for the area. They formed their own society and the only locals that became a part of the new leadership were the ones who sucked up to them.

No formal schools existed in the area as Will grew up, so some of his siblings went away to school. One day Will and his brother James were talking about their future.

"Well, Will Thomas, Mary Frances and Junior have all gone off for schooling and I guess I'm next. This leaves you as the oldest son at home. It'll be hard on you. After all you're only eight."

"I ain't going to no school. I'm going to stay right here. Ma and Pa will teach me all I need to know. Besides, why should I you're coming back and you can tell me what you learned."

"It wont be the same as if you go."

"Well I got more important things to thank about right now."

"You feel that way now , but I bet you change your mind later. If not you will surely live to regret it. So study on it before you decide for sure."

Later in life, Will found that James was right and wished he had heeded his advice. Had he been educated he would have been even more successful in life. If he had learned to read and write, his business dealings would have been easier to handle.

Despite the hardships the family endured. Will and his siblings had a good childhood. The family always ate together and after supper Milton and Elizabeth would tell stories about earlier times and how they came to Cherokee County. The kids loved to hear how their father had fulfilled their grandfather's dream of becoming a landowner and building a good home for the family.

WILL GROWS UP
CHAPTER II

On Sunday, after services at Salem Church. The congregation would gather at the Smith's house for socializing with stories, music and ice cream. People would bring fiddles, banjos and guitars to furnish music. Everyone knew their neighbors for miles around and they looked forward to these get-togethers each week.

As all were invited, these events also allowed new comers to the area and their children a chance to meet and get acquainted. At an early age, these gatherings were to change Will's life in ways he had only dreamed about before.

Will didn't like to admit it at first, but for some reason that he did not understand, he was attracted to girls. As with each boy, he soon learned why. His first puppy love was Jill Jackson when both were the tender age of twelve. One Sunday, she asked him to go behind the barn with her and once there asked him.

"Would you like to kiss me?"

Will was at a lose for words. He had never kissed a girl before. He finely uttered.

"Why would I want to kiss you?"

"I've seen my ma and pa do it and they sure seemed to like it. Every time they do they send me out to the barn to do chores."

Will had also seen his parents and now knew what to do.

Just as things were going right for Will, Jill's father came around the end of the barn. In a rough voice he yelled out.

"What are you two up to? Jill get back to the house and as for you Will Smith you stay away from her."

As he followed Jill back around the barn, he glanced back at Will and winked.

"Until the two of you are at least sixteen."

Will would now look forward to Sundays even more than before and as he aged he rapidly learned why. Farm boys and girls are constantly exposed to animals breeding. Thus, they are naturally curious about the mating habits of humans and some experiment with their own sexuality early in life.

Will and Jill learned a lesson on their first encounter. After that they found a better and less conspicuous place to be along. Each Sunday they would make sure that her ma and pa were occupied and then they would sneak away to explore the mysteries of life.

The Jackson family sharecropped for Will's father and was the Smith's closest neighbor. In 1885, Jill's father decided to move his family to Texas. His brother had done so earlier and had become successful as a storeowner. He wanted to buy a ranch and had asked his brother to come and work with him.

When Jill heard the news, she became very upset.

"**No**, I can't move away from Will. I'm sixteen now and you said he could court me when I was."

"Ma, your brother and me are going as for you and Will that

is up to you two."

Jill ran out the door and went in search of Will. She found him getting a team of oxen ready to deliver and ran to him crying.

"Will pa is moving the family to Texas and I don't want to go."

Will didn't know how to respond to this news. He held her for a while and then.

"Lets walk down by the spring. We can talk about it there."

As they walked hand in hand Jill suddenly turned to Will and blurted out.

"Will Smith I love you and don't want to leave you."

Will was at a loss for words. He sat down on a log and thought to himself.

"How am I going to get out of this."

He had never thought of their relationship as love before.

"I don't have a place of my own yet and you know how big ah family I've got. Could you go to Texas and soon as I can get us a place I'll come get you. Then we could get hitched."

Jill was both happy and sad. Will had never mentioned marriage before, but now he wanted her to go away for a while. She started to cry again and looking into Will's eyes,

"I will always love you no matter how far apart we may be."

Will saw his out.

"We'll write to each other and soon I'll come for you."

Jill smiled through her tears.

"Will Smith you don't know how to write. You never went to school."

"No but my brother can and he'll put down what I say. I won't forget you. One day you will look up and see me coming."

Jill pulled herself up to him and gave him a long lovers kiss. This set Will on fire and he thought to himself.

"Maybe I do care for her more than I thought."

Later, he walked Jill home and as they approached the house her Mother came out. She looked at them and smiled.

"You two come on in its suppertime."

Will had eaten there many times before but he was not ready for what was about to happen. After supper Jill's father turned to Will.

"Jill is of age now. Ma and me have always felt that when it was time you and Jill would get hitched. We know you two have been sneaking around for years now."

Jill flushed.

"Now pa you shouldn't say things like that."

She looked at Will and waited for a reaction, but once again Will was caught off guard. He thought about it for a while.

"Jill and I have discussed this. I will come and see you all in Texas in a year or so and then we'll see."

Jill's father frowned he now felt that Jill would never see Will again.

At this time, Will excused himself.

"I hope you all have a good trip to Texas."

He then took Jill out on the porch and kissed her.

"I'll miss you terribly but we will send letters to each other and I will see you next year."

As Will walked home, he thought to himself.

"Wow, I'd better be more careful. They almost trapped me and all I was doing was having fun."

Will had other intimate encounters as he grew into manhood but he tried to made sure that they were short lived affairs.

As many a young man does, Will decided to search out feminine companions a little further from home. On Saturday, he and his friend George would go into different towns in the surrounding area. They soon found plenty of girls who would fall for their charm and wit. By the time, he was eighteen, Will had quite a reputation as a ladies man.

One day in Tecumseh, Will met Alice Robershaw a beautiful

part Cherokee Indian. Alice was not immediately taken in by his charm. This was something different for him. At first he thought to heck with this one but it began to gnaw at him. He was not used to outright rejection and so devised a plan to conquer this hard to get girl. He talked another girl named Betty into having a social gathering at her home and inviting Alice. His plan did not seem to have worked as Alice mostly ignored him at this event.

He didn't know at the time that Betty had informed Alice of Will's intent. It was a well known fact that Will loved and left. Alice had made up her mind that she would teach him a thing or two. She rejected his advances and acted as though he bored her. She also had a plan of her own. She intended to have Will pursue her. Until, she caught him.

Will was now fascinated with this woman who paid him no attention. For the first time in his life, he found himself trying to gain a women's confidence.

Its impossible to say who caught whom but it worked out. Will and Sara Allis were married January 15, 1888. Allis gave Will eleven children Minnie Belle, Robert William, Elizabeth Ann, Mary Frances, Charles Boyd, Annie Laura Mae, James Thomas, Estelle Maria, Bessie Diana, Jacqueline and William Everett.

Will was a tall handsome man with black hair and blue eyes who never lost sight of the humble beginning from which he had descended. He was often called upon to mediate disputes between his neighbors as he was known to be a fair man who would show no favoritism. He was the type person that drew attention to himself without trying. This created many a problem from those jealous of him. They often expressed their feeling, "How dare this uneducated desperado exceed us in wealth."

Although without a formal education, Will ventured into several successful businesses. Some generally reserved for the well educated. He created charcoal pits and sold their product to mining companies, raised and sold oxen, goats, milk cows and pigs and used sharecroppers, to raise cotton and other crops. He lent money as in fact a one man unsanctioned loan company, bought and sold land and opened a General Store in Bluffton.. Will increased the Smith Family's land holdings to in excess of a thousand acres and his business ventures made them financially independent.

Will's businesses supported many families who worked for him. He was looked upon by the natives of Bluffton as a thoughtful and giving man. When a family found themselves in need of help due to ill health or other reasons they could depend on Will to come to their aid. He would provide food as well as money to help get them back on their feet. However; his success was frowned upon, by those who considered themselves the elite in the area.

During Will's life, the area in which he lived would go through many ups and downs. Events he witnessed were bound to dictate to some degree the type man he became.

There was a great abundance of iron ore in Cherokee County. Four furnaces were built to mine and smelt the ore into pig iron ingots. Bluffton the largest city in the County came into existence in the mid 1800's and then began to disappeared soon after the turn of the century. At its peak from the 1880s through the early 1900s, it was a boomtown of over eight-thousand residents. It was known as the Pittsburgh of the South. City officials planned for a city of over fifty-thousand, residents by the year 1900.

MAP
OF
BLUFFTON,
TOWNSHIP 6 RANGE 11 EAST
CHEROKEE CO.
ALA.

In 1890, Bluffton was a thriving city of approximately 8,000 residents. There was an e
generating plant, a water works, churches, a newspaper, a hotel, a school, and a pos
ncorporated businesses included the Bluffton Land, Ore and Furnace Company; the A
Arms Company; the Signal Land and Improvement Company; the Bluffton C
Company; and the Newark Land Company. The photograph shows a small portion of a
he town accomplished by the J.F. Falconnet Company from Nashville, TN. The map
March 1890.

The University of the Southland was planned for Bluffton and city officials donated $
to get it started. Its estimated construction cost was approximately $2 million. The archi
plans were compared to West Minister Abbey of England. A ground-breaking took pla
24, 1889, with dignitaries from all over the country in attendance. However, due to th
of iron ore mines, the college was never built.

By 1890, Bluffton had the first electrical generating plant in Cherokee County, a waters works system, a newspaper, hotel, churches, school and Post Office. The Bluffton Land, Ore and Furnace Company had purchased around 1,500 acres. They were selling houses as fast as they could build them. This companies Capital Stock was valued at $1,000,000.

Many businesses were established there. Signal Land & Improvement Company built houses, sold and mortgaged real estate. Bluffton Carwheel Company manufactured all articles large and small made from iron. The American Arms Company manufactured rifles, furniture, wagons, bicycles and many other items. In all, there were eleven manufacturing plants in town all of them plus other businesses were owned by northerners. The only business in town not owned by someone from the north was a General Store owned by William A. Smith.

Bluffton seemed on its way to becoming one of the most important cities of North America. Then misfortune struck. The ore fields did not meet hoped for expectations. The ore was of a poorer grade than that found near Birmingham and there was less of it. The foundries shutdown, the college was not built, jobs became scarce and people followed the jobs. Without a sufficient number of customers, businesses began to fail. The dreams faded away along with the town of Bluffton.

The East Tennessee, Virginia and Georgia Railroad built a main line through Bluffton which ran from New York to New Orleans. This was the beginning, of Will's problems with the Governor. The State of Alabama needed the railroad in order to keep up with the times and to transport the states goods to outside markets.

WILL'S LEGEND BEGINS
CHAPTER III

The Governor made agreements with the railroad that effected Will and his neighbors without their consent.

Several times actions by the railroads led to a financial loss to those whose land it crossed. After the railroad built a dam which backed water up over several acres of his farmland Will sued and was awarded damages against the railroad. This led to a rash of successful lawsuits against the railroad by Will and his neighbors. The railroad complained to the Governor about Will and he was designated a desperado and troublemaker.

Many stories have been written about Will Smith. These tales have been highly exaggerated, according to family members and others who knew him personally. He was a good businessman and generous to people in lack of the basic necessities. When a family was in need he would provide food and money to help get them back on their feet. He was often called upon to mediate disputes between his neighbors. He bothered no one. However, when confronted with a fight he never backed down.

Although; it is impossible to know the day to day ventures of Will Smith. It is possible to trace certain aspects of his life from official court records. Will was indicted and charged with killing one Joseph Hackney by shooting him with a pistol in December, of 1890. He was not ordered arrested by the Circuit Court Judge until July 11th, 1892. The trial was held later that month and the jury brought in a unanimous decision of not guilty.

July 30, 1892, Will was once again arrested and charged with the 1890 murder of Joseph Hackney. (Note: He had

already been tried and found innocent of this crime.)
He was indicted August 1, 1892 and held, for nineteen days, before bond was set and he was released. The case was continued until Jan 25, 1893. At this point the court ordered, "This case be not pressed as it has already been tried once and Will Smith was found innocent."

Those who had Will arrested again were trying to convince the court to ignore the Constitution of the United States which prohibits a re-trial of a person already found innocent of that crime. It's called Double Jeopardy.

August 10, 1892, Will's father; Milton Smith got into an alteration with two men who owed him money. He walked into a local business and confronted the men asking when they intended to pay their debt. An argument ensued and one of the men physically attacked Milton. They scuffled and Milton knocked him to the floor. The other man had separated himself from the fight. He drew a pistol and when Milton turned to face him he fired twice hitting Milton in the chest and head. The two left town and were never charged with the murder.

The selling of alcoholic beverages was illegal in Alabama thus bootlegging became a viable business. Will Smith gained the nickname Belltree when he hung a bell with a ringing rope from the limb of a large oak tree and created a Blind Tiger from which whiskey could be purchased.

Will's widowed sister owned and ran the Blind Tiger as a means of supporting herself. The buyer would place his money down on a stump, ring the bell and leave. After a while, he would return and his money would be gone. Whiskey and his change were in its place. The word got around and since it was on his land , Will was given the nickname of Belltree Smith.

The Belltree became so well known, this method of selling whiskey was immortalized in the song "White Lightening." The whiskey sold at this Blind Tiger was not however White Lightening. It was bonded liquor shipped from the Northeastern United States where it was legal. Several individuals who lived during Will's time told their children this and they passed it on to present day family members. However, after Will's death other Smiths did sell White Lightening.

Articles have been written stating that, "a customer was killed if he did not follow the rules." Also, articles have been written saying, "Belltree held card games at the tree, killing anyone who won his money." As you can see, if the card games had taken place, this would have broken the so-called rules. The quotes in the first two sentences of this paragraph are pure nonsense. Common sense tells you, if they were true no one would go there, thus no customers, no sales and no business.

Will Smith had many friends and acquaintances in Rome, Georgia. Among them were Doctor Robert Battey, Doctor William Harbin, Doctor Robert Harbin and the Berry family. It is well known that Will made healthy contributions to medical facilities and other good causes. The doctors were said to have spent many a day hunting on Will's land. The ones telling the story usually laugh when asked what they were hunting, but do not answer the question.

There is much evidence pointing to Will as a womanizer. He had two women at his home besides his wife. It is said that one was the family nurse and the other was a house servant. Several women also lived in cabins throughout Will's land. Some were widows and the others, who knows.

A well documented medical operation was performed by the

Harbin brothers on Will's land and paid for by him, in 1906.

It came to Will's attention that an elderly member of one of his sharecropper families had a growth so large on her stomach that she was carrying it around in a wheelbarrow. Will visited the lady and found the story to be true. He immediately sent for a doctor.

After examining the women, Doctors William and Robert Harbin determined it was a huge cyst and decided to operation. The procedure was performed on the lady's kitchen table. The patient survived and lived several years after the ordeal.

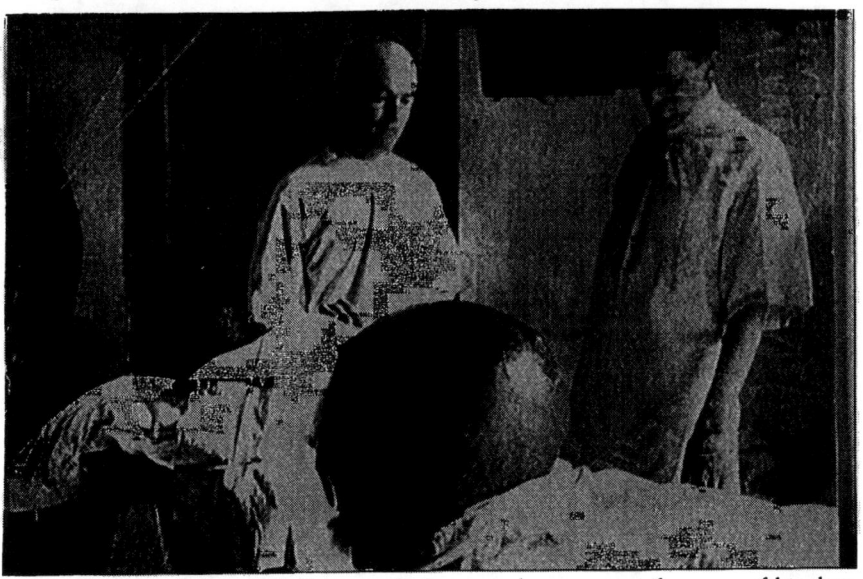

In 1906, William Smith of Bluffton was made aware that a woman from one of his share cropping families had a large tumor. Upon investigating, he discovered that her stomach was so large that she was carrying it around in a wheelbarrow. He sent for Drs. William P. and Robert M. Harbin of Rome, GA. The doctors performed an operation on the woman's kitchen table and successfully removed a giant cyst. The lady survived and lived for several more years.

Much has been written saying Will killed, depending on the article you read, various numbers of men. The only killing, of which documentation has been found, is his arrest for the murder of Joseph Hackney. He was tried and acquitted of this crime. This writer remembers as a youth listening to elderly family members talk about two men Will supposedly shot. The story goes as follows.

An elderly black couple lived on Will's land. One day, two drunken hunters came to their house. The men ordered the woman to cook them something to eat. She told them alright but that her husband would have to go outside and get some wood for the stove. They told the man to go and he did. The intruders sat down at the table and began to drink more whiskey and the woman began preparing to cook. After a while, when the husband did not come back, one of the men.

"He's gone for Belltree."

They jumped up and went out onto the porch. At this time, the husband and Will were approaching the house. One of the drunken men raised his shotgun and fired. Belltree drew his pistol and shot the man between the eyes. The other then started to shoot, but was killed before he could. This story may or may not be true and I am sure if it is true it has been embellished from the original happenings. True or not it makes a good story, doesn't it? It is far more believable than other poorly researched writings about William A, (Belltree) Smith.

A GOOD MAN IS MURDERED
CHAPTER IV

Will recognized the handicap a lack of education had placed on him and made sure that his children went to school. He also ensured that their other needs were met.

A man such as described in the previous paragraphs is bound to create enemies and Will Smith had more than his share. Despite being a man of means, he was never written about in newspapers of his day except in a degrading manner. Even his death has been reported in so many distorter ways it is hard to decipher the truth from the fiction. The newspaper story which appeared the most often and is the same as that told by family members is as follows.

"In Sept of 1908, during an all day singing and dinner at a church in Borden Springs, Alabama an encounter between Will and the Chandler Brothers ended with Will being shot and killed. As Will left the church he was passing by the railroad station when he notice two men attacking his brother. He immediately dismounted and assisted his brother. While he was busy thrashing one of the attackers a third man hit him from behind with a rock and while he was disorientated Will Chandler pulled a pistol and shot Will Smith in the head."

Will Chandler was arrested and tried for the murder. Although found guilty he never served even a day of his sentence. The Governor (who it was rumored akin to Chandler) immediately gave him a full pardon. Chandler left the area and was seen years later at a resort living as only a wealthy man could. Was he paid to kill Smith? No one alive today could know.

William Smith was well off financially and respected among

the general populace but he was not accepted by the so called In Crowd. They called him a desperado. It was obvious; many were glad he was dead.

The following was extracted from the Cleburne News printed Sept 26, 1908.

"Will Chandler was placed on trial here last Wednesday for the killing of Will Smith. The jury, after having been out only a few minutes, brought in a verdict of manslaughter. Within thirty minutes after the jury rendered its verdict, all the jurors, <u>solicitors</u> and the judge had signed a petition asking the Governor to grant him a pardon."

The petition had been prepared in advance of the trial as was the pardon. Does this not smell of a prearranged murder by the Governor, Judge, lawyers and others? Justice was truly blind in this case.

William Siglin, Justice of Peace, was assigned as executor of William A. Smith's estate. He reported that Will owned 1060 acres of land plus his 160 acre homestead and was half owner of 175 more acres. Siglin collected debts owed to Will and deposited this money along with cash left by Will. This amounted to $10,859,35. A sizable amount in 1908. He also listed a large number of farm items and livestock owned by Will.

The administrator, William Siglin also stated in his report.

"Amount of claims against the estate still unpaid <u>nothing.</u>"

It has been said that Will had bank accounts in other counties not found by the state administrator. True or false, who knows, this writer doesn't.

This writing tells an abbreviated story of the life of William Anderson (Belltree) Smith, it has been laid out before you the reader. Now <u>you</u> be the judge. Desperado or just a victim who bucked the system and lost. Be assured, many others have already judged him from made up tales by people who did not bother to properly research before writing or talking about him.

YOU CAN SURVIVE

AMERICA'S FINAL

WAR

INTRODUCTION

World happenings today are truly leading down the path described within this book. It is a book of death but also of survival against incredible odds. Only those properly prepared will be alive ten years from today. Will you be one of them? Reading this book may increase your chances.

This book is partially fiction as no one can predict the future but many of the events are real and have already occurred. Most of us are helpless in preventing our own destruction, but in this book Will Ferguson shows how you may survive the coming war.

Man is destroying life as it is in the early twenty-first century. Will Ferguson foresees America's most disastrous war coming. It will span the Northern Hemisphere and at its end few people and only a small number of nations will have survived.

This book takes a reader from the events of today and transports him well into the future.

God granted man the precious gift of life and
Man ever since in the name of God has
sought ways to end life soon they
may achieve near total success
in this quest.

**Will -- You -- Survive
America's Final War**

Copyright 2002

AMERICA'S FUTURE
CHAPTER ONE

The United States is a thing of the past. Few American's survived the nation's Final War. The military and government no longer exist. Although most government officials had been in well constructed and stocked shelters. The majority of these havens had received direct hits. Those not killed by the blast were buried alive as the entrances were covered by thousands of tons of rock from the hollowed out mountains the shelters were built in. Those who survived found there was almost no one to govern. Other shelters were not properly constructed and were unable to protect their inhabitants. While still others had not been properly stocked with food and water. This forced the people to either venture outside before it was safe or starve, either way meant certain death.

By 2015, North America was safe for those who survived to leave their shelters. Those near cities were stunned at what they saw. The structures were demolished and there was devastation everywhere. No life forms could be found. It is very disturbing that there appears to be nothing nor no one alive and most structures were in ruin.

Years later Gary Ferguson talks to his Grandson. Who asks, "Grandpa what happened? Where are the people and big buildings we see when we watch the old movies."

"Jake lets sit under that little oak tree and I will tell you how your Great Grandfather Will Ferguson's view of the future saved the Ferguson's and many others."

The following is his story.

"The United States was once the mightiest power on

earth. Their influence was felt world wide. For many years they had pursued the friendship of nations by assisting them financially and militarily when deemed necessary. This appeared to work with most governments as the officials there used most of the moneys for their own benefit. However; this only fostered hate and resentment against the United States. Without revealing it, these same officials felt the American's were interfering with their internal affairs. The money was intended to raise the standard of living for the general populace. However ; little was used for that and the local government officials told their people that it was America's interfering that caused their suffering. Thus hatred against Americans spread throughout much of the world. Many countries in Western Europe, Asia and Africa eventually explode into violence against the United States."

A Secret Army of renegades Muslims was formed with the destruction of America as their goal. Undercover moles were in place throughout the world by 1996. Individual members were not informed as to the names of other agents. They were never to try and contact anyone about their mission. They had been trained and indoctrinated in the actions each was to take during the declared Holy War against all Christian and Hebrew nations. They came from many backgrounds and social levels. The common thread that drew them together was their hatred for the United States and Israel. Using this hatred, self appointed leaders banded them together, brainwasher them and formed an army of millions. The world had never before known the likes of this army.

Most of their leaders were trained by America's military and educated in American Colleges. They knew that to attack America directly would only lead to their elimination so they decided to slowly infiltrate all facets of America's society.

The army was not named only different units of it were. If one unit was discovered, its members could not identify the entire army. For security purposes, only the top people knew who the leaders of other units were or the goal of each unit. One unit, Al Quida openly trained the militants necessary for combat actions and suicide missions.

Soldiers in civilian clothing migrated from many countries but most came from the Middle East. The moles training had taken place in such a none conspiratorial fashion as it drew little attention from local governments. They infiltrated all levels and branches of their targeted countries society. Members became teachers in schools and colleges throughout the world. Their mission was to slowly brainwash the students against the United States. Those in America taught hatred for the government.

In a few years, they appeared to be outstanding citizens. Pillows of their community. Many were family men and placed their children in local schools. They and their wives joined clubs and participated in social functions. During the years of waiting on the call to perform their assigned mission, they masked their hatred well. They either were or trained to become pilots, doctors, newsmen, and a variety of other professions. Some even ran and were elected to public office. The penetration was so complete that one was a member of the Secret Service guarding the President of the United States.

Although from many different backgrounds, they had two things in common hatred for Americans and their religious beliefs. As men do, their leaders had interpreted religious writings to their personal advantage and brainwashed their followers into believing them right. Many were programmed as suicide weapons and others were trained to produce and use chemical, biological or nuclear weapons. They truly believed that if death was their mission they would then pass on directly to Heaven. Once there, they would be welcomed as hero's and have many privileges. One of the things they would be given was seven virgins for their pleasure.

Each was to wait patiently for notification to begin the mission against their assigned country. At what was considered the right time, the leaders would signal the start of their Holy War. Each was told not to react when other cells performed a military act unless they received orders to do so.

Major events against the United States and its allies began to occur more often throughout the world. Embassies, overseas military installations and military personnel residences were targeted by the secret cells. These attacks were meant to cause a military response by the United States against an Islamic government. This was then to be used as propaganda to recruit millions of others to join their ranks. The 1990's saw many acts of terrorism against the United States, Israel, India and several other nations but received little response from America's president. This was interpreted as a sure sign of weakness. The terrorist leaders decided that it was time to step up their offensive against the United States. It was deemed necessary to strike in a manner that would cause the United States to attack an Islamic nation. They speculated that such an attack would convince millions more to join in their Holy War.

Sept 11, 2001, started as an average day for most American's but they were about to be stunned into questioning the potential for their own survival. The entire nation was to feel what only the military had felt before. Each in their own way was awoken from their false feelings of security from outside forces. Most had become complacent and believed that no one would ever again attack the United States on its soil.

The attention of the entire world was about to shift to New York, City and Washington D. C.

A cell in the United States was ordered into action. Eight members had receive flight training while undercover. Only two had been previously identified as potential terrorist. They had checked airport security procedures over the previous months. It was decided that they would hijack two aircraft in Chicago, one in Washington D. C. and one in Newark. These would be their weapons of mass destruction. Without an incident, they easily boarded the aircraft with knives and box openers. Security had been as they had hoped, all but none existent.

These particular flights were chosen because they were bound from the east to the west coast and because of the distance would have a full load of fuel. Within minutes into each flight the terrorist were able to kill the cockpit crews and take command of the four aircraft. They then announced to the passengers that this was a hijack and if they just relaxed they would be okay.

Minutes later the first aircraft crashed into the North Tower of the World Trade Center. As firemen and police were attempting to evacuate the building and rescue the injured another aircraft crashed into the South Tower. Approximate fifty thousand people from sixty countries worked in the two towers. Because of the early hour most were not at work. At 10am the South Tower collapsed and twenty-nine minutes later the North Tower also came down. Another aircraft crashed into the Pentagon in Washington D. C. at the same time as the first hit a tower. At 10:10am, the fourth aircraft crashed in a wooded area Southeast of Pittsburgh.

The innocence of Americans came to an abrupt end. In a

short time, the events in New York and Washington became the most important thing in their lives. Many questions were asked. Foremost everyone wanted to know, is this just the start? When and where will the next attack take place? How were the hijackers able to bring weapons aboard four different aircraft at three different airports? Who planned and financed this action?

America's primary financial center came to a halt. America's Stock Market closed. Pictures of the towers falling were flashed around the world. Most that seen them did not want to believe this had happened. Many pressed the government for revenge.

The Television networks stopped all news coverage except for this event. Thousands of Palestinians were shown celebrating the attack and chanting, "God is great." They also showed Islamic children firing weapons in the air celebrating. Television became the voice of America's enemy. Reporting everything that was said against the United States. They did exactly as the Holy War leaders had hoped they would. Well meaning but misguided American college students formed peace marches against America's Government perhaps from brainwashing by their professors.

Years earlier Colonel Ollie North, testifying before a congressional committee, warned of the dangers America faced from terrorist. He was asked, "Who do you fear the most." He responded, "Osama bin Laden." His warning was laughed at and dismissed. Immediately following the attack on 9/11/02 many experts on terrorist and the Middle East were asked who they felt was most likely behind this attack to a man they said, "Osama bin Laden and his Al Quida network." This was the only highly visible unit of the secret army. It trained its militant recruits in camps known to all. Afghanistan's Taliban

Government welcomed them and their leader Osama bin Laden. Afghanistan had been involved in a Civil War for Years and the Al Quida fighters gave them the edge needed to maintain control of the country.

The leaders who ordered the attack on the World Trade Center met, laughed and bragged about the attack's success. It inflicted far more damage than they had hoped for. Osama bin Laden was laughing as he said, "Most of the hijackers did not know they were to die until minutes before they did. They thought it was only a hijack not a suicide mission." The fact that they had sent men to their death meant nothing to them and killing approximately three thousand people from sixty different nations was celebrated by them. They then waited for the response from the United States that was sure to come.

The leaders of the Secret Army were surprised at the actions taken by America's President. Instead of immediately striking back at a hastily targeted suspect nation, he put the entire United States on high alert, closed all major airports and ordered the call up of national guard units to protect potential high profile areas. He also ordered the Air Force to fly around the clock missions to intercept any other potential threats from the air and the Coast Guard to scrutinize all incoming ships. The ships were to be kept away from America's shores until they were fully checked and cleared.

After being informed by the Central Intelligence Agency and the Federal Bureau of Investigations that his predecessor had placed restrictions on them which made it hard to operate properly, the president rescinded those restrictions. He then ordered these agencies to use all available means to identify the planners of this attack on America. They were also instructed to uncover any other threats against the United States or its allies and deal with them appropriately.

The president waited patiently as intelligence was gathered. After making sure who the enemy was, he formed a Coalition of nations surrounding them. He convinced national leaders that terrorist were planning to overthrow their governments and used several examples to prove his point. The North Atlantic Treaty Organization immediately aligned with the United States and England became our strongest ally. The ones hunted turned out to be the ones suspected from the start Osama bin Laden and his Al Quida forces.

The Taliban Government of Afghanistan where bin Laden was residing refused to join the Coalition so the president requested that they arrest Osama bin Laden and turn him over to the United States for trial. The Taliban was deeply dependent upon bin Laden for financial and military support thus they refused to arrest him. Instead, they aligned themselves with him. It soon became apparent, the only way the United States could punish bin Laden was to destroy his terrorist camps and Al Quida organization and either capture or kill him.

The United States and England began bombing the terrorists camps, hideout caves and residents of known Al Quida leaders. The Taliban Army fired ground to air rockets at American and British aircraft. and because of this action, they were also targeted.

The Northern Alliance which was made up of several tribes had been fighting the Taliban since 1996. The bombings gave them a chance to advance and they attacked with everything they had. It became necessary for the United States and England to assist the Northern Alliance in overthrowing the Taliban Government. They did so by increasing the bombings on government officials residences and their army instillations. The United States poured billions of dollars into the countries within the war area who had joined with them in the coalition against terrorist.

The actions taken by the United States was far more severe than the Secret Army had anticipated but it did serve the purpose they had hoped for. Thousands of Muslims from all around the world joined them in their declared Holy War against the United States and its allies. Other terrorist acts were ordered in various parts of the world. Al Quida forces joined with rebels against Russia in Chechnya. American troops joined with the Government of the Philippines against rebelling Muslims there. Almost daily there were terrorist acts against Israel. Many other attempted acts of terrorism were foiled by the CIA, FBI and their counterparts in other countries. Near one-thousand terrorist were arrested before they could carry out their act of destruction.

In January of 2002, China led a six nation group in warning the United States not to attempt to influence Afghanistan's future. The president responded by warning Iran and all other nations not to harbor terrorist.

Grandpa Ferguson kept up with world events as best he could. The way most news reports were presented it was sometimes hard to decipher what was actually happening. Reporters followed each report with their own slanted view of what had happened. Will and most others felt that they did not need someone to tell them what they had just witnessed. His inward feelings told him that the United States was in serious trouble. His thoughts continued to warn him that an all out war was soon to come.

Will considered purchasing a factory manufactured survival shelter but decided against it. After examining several, he concluded they would only be a coffin for those within them.

One day as if instructed by a divine power, Will began to sketch plans for a survival shelter. It was soon obvious that when he finished the drawings he could never afford to build the structure. However; something kept urging him to complete them. He also felt he must build a model and test its strength.

In 2003, intelligence sources identified Iraq as having the potential to manufacture and distribute weapons of mass destruction. This led to Operation Desert Storm, a war which removed Iraq's Anti-American Government. The swiftness with which Afghanistan and Iraq were conquered and the arrest of many of their operatives throughout the world delayed the Secret Army's plans temporarily. However; this also gave fuel to their propaganda against all Christian and Hebrew nations allowing them to recruit millions of new Moslem followers.

In 2010, the Secret Army felt their numbers were sufficient to start and win Civil Wars in several countries and ordered their sleepers to action. All out war began throughout the Middle East, Asia and Africa. Many governments were overthrown and the United States was unable to prevent this as the actions were internal affairs for each country.

Will watched with awe as each country fell to the Secret Army. Terrorist acts continued and America's Final War drew nearer with each act against the United States or their allies and with America's response to them.

WAR IS UPON US
CHAPTER TWO

By 2009, Will was convinced a world war was eminent. He had been researching in earnest the type shelter required for his family to survive. He used the public library in Rome, Georgia and the internet to locate and record all available data. His findings were discouraging. The shelter must protect against chemical, biological and nuclear attack for an extended period of time. To accomplish this it must have walls and a roof capable of withstanding the initial blast with its earthquake like tremor and intense heat.

The shelter must have its own ecosystem. The internal air must be recycled to provide the fresh oxygen essential to sustain life. Sufficient food and unpolluted water must be available and waste disposal was a major concern.

Since it looked as though he could never raise the funds needed, Will decided to plan a shelter that would not only support life but would do so in a comfortable manner. He began to modify his original design, searching for what he hoped would be the perfect structure. He drew plans for different types of shelters, evaluating each for its survival potential.

It was obvious that to plan a shelter only large enough for Will's family would never do because it would be impossible to keep it a secret. Once construction permits were requested many would know about it. Will wants to save as many people as possible and he knows he would have trouble turning anyone away once the war started. It was however; a sure thing that if too large a crowd crammed into a tight space chances were no one would survive. He decides to list it as an underground house.

In January of 2010, Will settles on the shelter plan he hopes will do all that's required of it. It calls for a concrete and steel dome shaped structure with three levels. In the center, there is a hollow column twenty feet in diameter with twelve inch steel I-beams spaced every four feet and reaching from the floor to the ceiling. Stairs, a water well and water treatment plant are located in the center of this column. The entire dome is covered with several feet of dirt and sodded with grass to prevent erosion. Properly built the shelter is designed to house approximately one-hundred people for a substantial period of time.

Will also designed a smaller domed shelter. It has most of the features of the larger one and could provide protection for up to fifty people. Perhaps this would help prevent overcrowding of the main shelter. He must now pray for funds to built two shelters instead of one.

Will had previously considered building a tornado shelter within the hill behind his house. This now seemed the perfect place for the newly planned war shelters, providing funds became available to do so. The mountain across from his house would provide potential protection if a nuclear blast occurred either West or Northwest of his location and a large hill would serve that purpose to the Southeast. He knew there were many mountains and hills between his location and the most likely targets in his area.

The many Government facilities in Huntsville, Alabama and the millions of people in and around Atlanta, Georgia seemed to point to them as prime targets for ICBM attack. Atlanta was seventy miles to the southeast and Huntsville was over a hundred miles Northwest from the Ferguson's property. The mountains would only provide partial protection and none if a missile missed its target and struck too close to the shelter.

Will deducted his current home would provide no protection from radiation fallout or chemical and biological contamination. The only way for the Ferguson family to survive was to somehow raise the funds necessary to build a proper shelter. He estimated it would cost between ten and twelve million dollars to construct and stock the two shelters. He also knew time was running out.

Each day the world situation seemed to worsen. By February 2010, Will was sure World War III was coming and soon. Most people now felt war would happen and many in panic began looking for a way to survive it. Will decided to place his plans for sale on the internet and with television advertisements. A cutaway model was used in the ads to show the shelters potential. Will offered to furnish a Supervisor of Construction with each shelter built to insure the structures met his standards. The more shelters properly built the more Americans that would survive the war. He suggested strongly that the structures be built inside hills or mountains at least fifty miles from a major city or other area prime for attack. Will stipulated that these supervisors would only be available for shelters built within fifty miles of his own. He did not want any family member far from home as it was impossible to know exactly when to enter and stay inside a shelter.

The thing that bothered Will the most was that only the rich could afford to construct a shelter. He consoled himself by knowing the rich would also take in people as servants to look after their needs.

The Ferguson family was surprised by the response from the advertisements. Within a month they had sold sufficient numbers to begin construction of their own shelter. At this point, Will offered the plans for a very low price. Perhaps individuals who could not afford a shelter could form groups and do so. He now prayed there would be sufficient time to complete the construction of the shelters.

June 2010, The first structure begin to take shape and was completed by mid April 2011. The shelter was built deep enough inside the hill to provide three rooms in a main hall which led into the dome. These rooms could only be entered through airlock type steel doors remotely operated from a Security Control Room or inside the rooms themselves using manual handles. Once the war started, anyone entering the shelter must follow strict rules before they were allowed to enter the main shelter.

When anyone entered cameras and an intercom system would monitor the process and insure each individual followed procedure. Once inside the first room , all contaminated clothing were to be discarded. Next comes the shower and decontamination room. After decontamination, they enter a dressing room and clothe themselves in white robes provided for them. After dressing they enter the medical area where they undergo a physical examination. This procedure was primarily meant to protect the inhabitants of the shelter from anything entering that might endanger their health. Once the war started no one would be allowed to bring anything inside with them. Essential items they would need was already stored there.

As soon as the main shelter was ready, the Ferguson family began to stock it and gather the personnel needed to inhabit their new underground city. A family doctor, dentist, plumber, schoolteacher, electronics technician and their immediate families were already listed as shelter residents. This group plus Will's family would fill the shelter almost to capacity. Will wanted life to continue as close to normal as possible for those inside. His plans include a list of items necessary for approximately one-hundred people to survive for several years and instructions on how to maintain a livable atmosphere over this period.

The shelter was stocked and everyone was waiting for the right time to move into the shelter. Will decides that once the war starts no one will be turned away until allowing more to enter would endanger the lives of those already inside. He also wrote rules by which the residents must abide. These started off with God's Ten Commandments and setup a procedure to insure no individual did anything foolish which would endanger others. Anyone not obeying the laws would be banished to the outside. Anyone wishing to leave was free to do so but if someone did leave they would not be allowed to re-enter.

Sufficient funds became available to begin construction of a smaller shelter near the first and it was started immediately. Will prayed for enough time to complete this one. When completed the extended families of those in the original shelter and others could hopefully be safe there.

By December 2010, everyone knew the name of the Secret Army. It calls it's self Dar-al Harb (The Abode of War). This army now controls most of the Middle East and parts of Africa and Asia. They announced their goal as, "The ruling to kill the Americans and their allies-civilian and military-is an individual duty of every Muslim who can do it in any country in which it is possible to do it." They stopped shipping oil and all other normally exported goods to the United States and its allies. Then convinced others to do the same. It did not bother these jihad (Holy War) leaders that these actions would cause undue hardships on their own people. They used this to their advantage by convincing the general populace that the United States was responsible for their suffering. Many more joined their ranks. Even those who did agree with their policies had little choice as for many it was join the military or starve.

The United States and its NATO allies find all at once few are friendly toward them. China has waited decades for the opportunity to destroy America. It now sees its chance and aligns with these new governments against the United States. Russia increases oil sales to the United States and joins NATO. It becomes a strong ally as they are also under continuing terrorist attacks.

America's economy is in bad shape. Many are unemployed and protest against the military and government grow. All NATO allies are also suffering from a weak economy and continuous terrorist attacks. Many goods that had helped fuel business are no longer available for import. Gloom seems to hang over the whole world. Most are now convinced there is no way to prevent a world war.

The FBI and CIA have identified and arrested hundreds of terrorist but the ACLU and antiwar groups complain heavily to the government that these people are being denied their right to free speech and life style. Thousands march on Washington demanding the prisoners be released.

July 4, 2011, a mole within the Secret Service shoots the president of the United States and assassination attempts are made on all NATO countries leaders. Many are killed, but the President and two others survive the attacks. The president is seriously wounded and the Vice-President assumes control of the country. New leaders are immediately sworn in to lead the other NATO countries. America's acting President Wyatt places the nation on red alert, activates all National Guard and reserve units and the other NATO countries call their reserves to active duty.

Thousands of men and women in all NATO countries join the armed forces. Current events do not allow time for proper training. With little training, most are put in uniform and used to try and control rioting and looting that is now wide spread. As things worsen wide spread desertion becomes a major problem among the new recruits.

Terrorist cells in all NATO countries including the United States are activated. During their years of blending in as ordinary citizens, the terrorist have been able to manufacture and store within the United States large quantities of chemical/biological weapons and dirty bombs (small nuclear weapons). Water systems are poisoned, chemicals are sprayed over wide areas and terrorist placed nuclear bombs explode in key cities in the United States and NATO countries.

President Dollar's wife and Staff Aide Bill are with him at the underground hospital as the doctor talks to him.

"We have successfully removed the bullet. It punctured your right lung and did other damage. You will fully recover if we can insure no infection sets in. I will keep you here for a week or so."

"Where is the Vice-President?"

"He is in the War Room. I have advised him of your condition. It looks bad most of the other world leaders were not as lucky as you."

"Take me to the War Room"

"You cannot be moved for at least another twenty-four hours."

"BILL, LAURA get me to the War Room now."

"If you do this, I am not responsible for what might happen."

Bill is discussed by the doctors comment.

"None of us may be alive tomorrow and you worry about your responsibility. JUST STAND CLEAR."

Bill and Laura then roll the presidents bed to the elevator and down to the War Room. When he enters he surprises all present. The Vice-President looks at the President.

"Frank what are you doing? The doctor called and said you could bleed to death if your internal stitches break loose."

The president doesn't answer to this instead.

"Give me a quick briefing.?

"It looks bad Israel is under heavy ground and air attack. Terrorist have exploded dirty bombs in New York City, Washington D.C. and other key locations. Water has been contaminated and chemicals have been sprayed over wide areas. China is condemning us as the aggressor and I fear its only a matter of days before they launch on us."

"We must not be caught in the same location. Jerry take Sara and board the Airborne command Center. If word comes of incoming, fly south to Mexico. One of us must survive and they are still friendly to us."

The president then turns his attention to General Franklin the War Room Commander.

"General, order all overseas military to retreat to the closest friendly country and the entire Navy out to sea. Are our ships and subs positioned off the enemies coast?"

"Yes Sir. They await your command."

At 0600 hrs, General Franklin wakes the president.

"Sir, Israel and all NATO nations including Russia are reporting incoming ICBM's from several Middle East and African countries. They are retaliating and firing their entire nuclear arsenal."

Then after a short moment. The general shouts.

"SIR, we have incoming from China, from the sea and their mainland."

President Dollar has anticipated this and with a very heavy heart.

"Order the Air Force airborne and notify the Vice-President to fly south. Order our Air Force and Navel Fleet to fire upon their designated targets and then head south at flank speed. Is our missile defense system operational? If we are lucky it will stop some of the incoming."

"Your orders are being carried out as we speak. As for the Missile Defense System, it has been activated. What there is of it. I wonder what those who placed their own concerns over the welfare of the nation and continued to cause delays in its implementation are thanking now?"

The United States had worked since the 1980's to develop a missile defense system but short sighted politicians worried more about their own re-election than the future welfare of the nation had continually caused delays. At first they scared the general public by calling it Star Wars and a waste of money. Finely in 2010, sufficient money was made available to place the system in service, alas too late, and only a small number of satellite anti-missile missiles were in place.

Several incoming ICBM's are destroyed, but the majority get through. The missiles that strike the United States have warheads of either a cluster of 200 megaton nuclear bombs, or chemical and biological agents. Most people not killed by the initial nuclear blasts become victims of radiation fallout, chemical agents or biological viruses.

The world as it was at the start of the twenty-first century is gone forever. The United States is completely destroyed. Few will survive America's Final War.

THE SHELTER IS OCCUPIED
CHAPTER THREE

When the news that the president had been shot reached Will, He decided the time has come to begin entering the shelter. He sends out the word to assemble there. Within hours many on the list had arrived and gathered within their new sanctuary.

Scenting the inevitable the Munoz side of Will's family had left from Texas heading to Georgia two days earlier. Other relatives lived near the Mexican border and had decided to go south deep within Mexico as the war was not expected to spread there. They had converted all the dollars they could raise into Mexican pesos and left for Acapulco the week before.

Doctor Reeves brings his wife to the shelter, but he does not stay. He tells his family.

"I love each of you, but I am a doctor sworn to aid the sick. I am needed at the hospital more than here."

Will tries to talk him out of leaving

A Security team led by Will's son Joe was in place before most enter the shelter. Joe remotely controls the entrance doors and monitors all actions from a secure Control Room on the second level. Camera's placed at strategic points allow a 360 degree view of inside and outside the shelter. Some of the medical staff are the first to enter. Joe had positioned men to direct everyone into the hospital where they were given a fast checkup by the medical team. People formed a line and waited to be cleared. Two showed signs of being sick and were placed in isolation until a complete physical could be given.

Will and two of his sons Bobby and Gary were near the entrance to watch for late arrivals, maintain order and give instructions to families as they arrived. Since no missiles had as of yet struck the area, everyone was allowed to enter without being required to decontaminate.

Many had entered when a loud explosion is heard from the direction of Rome and the ground begins to shake beneath their feet. Will rushes the remaining people inside and using the intercom tells Joe, "Close the outside doors, secure the shelter and close the camera covers." Within a half hour several more blast were felt. Joe, "They have just hit Atlanta. All Atlanta television stations are off the air. We were monitoring Channel 2, 5,10, 11 and CNN as the shock waves hit. They kept the camera's on until the end. Nothing can be alive there."

Will, Bobby and Gary then survey for damage to the shelter. People are shaken but no one is seriously hurt and only minor damage had occurred. Will had made the decision to occupy the shelter in the nick of time. Obviously one intercontinental ballistic missile had missed its intended target and exploded nearby. To move inside at any later date would have been too late for many who were now protected.

Will contacted shelter two and asked for a report. Henry the Shelter Chief, "There is minor damage from the blasts but nothing serious. One person was hurt from a falling object and is being treated for his injury. Twenty people have entered the shelter so far." Will, "We have around sixty here. Keep me informed if more arrive and be sure everyone who enters from now on is decontaminated. Inform everyone of the shelters rules for survival and stress how strictly they will be enforced......... Since you are not fully stocked you must ration as you see fit. We will not try the tunnel between us until we are sure the war is over. We are monitoring it and it has caved in part way down the passageway. I guess from the tremors. In a week or so, we will try to open it. That's all for now."

The lights suddenly go out and Joe flips the switches which start the shelter's own electrical system and disconnects from the outside source. Even though battery operated emergency lights came on when the electricity was temporarily lost, some people began to panic.

Over the public address system, Joe orders them to calm down and be quiet. He is monitoring several television networks over cable and satellite systems. The cable goes dead, so he transfers satellite reception to large screens in the assembly and medical areas. Everyone watches and listens to news of the world crumbling around them. Joe is unable to locate a single station in the United States or Europe still on the air. All signals still operating were in foreign languages except one which was transmitting from Northern Canada. The report from this station temporally sent those watching into silent shock.

Once everyone is assembled, Will asks Joe to turn off the television. He then addresses the group, "The blast we felt was obviously a powerful nuclear bomb which exploded nearby. We may experience more ground shaking in the next couple of days. The war will then be over. There will be no winner for as you have just seen most countries including the United States no longer exist. I am happy to report the shelter suffered no major damage from this invasion. I now feel we are safe------at least for now.

The television will be left on twelve hours daily for as long as we can receive a station. Our primary electrical system has sufficient fuel for approximately two years of operation. If it becomes necessary to stay inside longer, we have two backup systems. We shall not waste electricity. The power will be shutoff in all areas except the Control Room each night at 2300hrs, unless a significant event occurs. The power will be restored each morning at 0600hrs in the early kitchen staff's rooms and 0700hrs everywhere else. There are flashlights in each sleeping area use them only when absolute necessary as we have a limited supply of replacement batteries.

When the power is shut down emergency lights will come on as long as the rechargeable batteries last. These lights are located in the main lobby only. There is an intercom in every room which is connected to the Control Room. These are to be used only for announcements from the Control Room or in emergencies.

We have sufficient food and other supplies to last for several years if necessary. I pray it will not be that long. Food will be rationed to the kitchen only. Everyone will receive three meals a day as long as supplies last. There is a personal items store, these items will also be rationed. Each room is already furnished with a supply of toiletries and several white robes.

The robes will be our primary clothing as long as we are here. I suggest that you save the clothes you were wearing when you entered and wear them when we leave. A laundry is available and everyone will be responsible for cleaning their own clothing and the other items in their area.

There are a lot of tasks to be accomplished and everyone will either volunteer or be assigned one. Money is no good here and there are no social classes. Everyone is equal and our survival depends upon each of us doing his or her part. We will face many problems and must work together to overcome them."

Someone shouts out.

"You say the world is ending and you talk to us about assignments."

"It is true the world as we have known it has disappeared. We can accept our chance for survival and maybe start over or we can just give up, go outside and die. Each of you made the choice to come here no one forced you. You must have felt that here you and your family have a chance to survive. Few of you contributed to the construction or stocking of equipment and supplies. The way I see it you have no right what so ever to complain about the conditions in which we will be forced to live.

Anyone who does not wish to work with the rest of us on this are welcome to leave anytime they wish. However, if you do decide to leave you will not be allowed to return. If you decide to stay, become an agitator, incite problems and make a general nuisance of yourself you will be forcibly removed from the shelter. Our temporary world must function as a small town where everyone does their share. If anyone does not, they go to jail and our jail is outside the shelters protection.......... The words I have just been forced to say were harsh but I said them for the good of all and I pray to God that everything runs as smooth as possible under our circumstances. I suggest we all work together and perhaps God will help us make it through our ordeal.

We will be testing the outside environment daily and as soon as it is safe to do so we will all go out. The Control Room will also be monitoring the outside for any activity. Anyone wishing to visit the control room are welcome to do so. I recommend that each of you visit on a regular schedule. Besides the outside cameras, the room is also equipped with a short wave radio and is constantly in touch with other survivors in shelters like this one. These visits will help you to understand why we must wait until it is safe before venturing out. However; because of the size of the room, you must make an appointment ahead of time. Only six people will be allowed to enter at a time and the visits will be limited to thirty minutes.

Unless the camera's become damaged, we can monitor a constant view of the entire surrounding area as each camera transmits to a different screen.

Breakfast will be served from 0800 until 0900hrs, lunch from 1200 to 1300hrs and dinner from 1900 until 2000hrs. A buzzer will sound ten minutes before a meal is to be served. Please try to be on time and do not tie up the kitchen staff any longer than necessary. Anyone who fails to show up during these hours without a good excuse will have to wait until the next meal in order to eat.

We have over a thousand movies on DVD's. A different movie will by shown each night beginning at 2000hrs here in the assembly area. There is also a well stocked library for your reading pleasure. For children from the first grade through the twelve grade, school hours are from 0915 until 1500hrs Monday through Friday. The school is in one room with one teacher so she will need several volunteer helpers.

A fishpond stocked with fingerlings is located on the first level. As you can see there are plants in abundance throughout the shelter. These will help provide oxygen. There are many other features here that I have not mentioned. Much thought has gone into bringing as much of our former life inside as possible.

Most of you have been here before and are already assigned sleeping quarters. The rest of you will be shown your bedrooms after this meeting. Place your name on the assigned quarters and then rest for a while. It is now 1400hrs at 1900hrs everyone please come to the dining area for dinner. We will have a short meeting after the meal with a question and answer period. Each of you who do not already have an assignment can look at the list and pick one. We will each work only as many hours as is required to accomplish our task. Most can be accomplished in a few hours daily. This meeting is now adjourned."

Bobby , "Those already assigned quarters go there now and please mark your door so we will know who all is in the shelter. The rest of you assemble with your families to the left of this area. Gary and I will show you to your quarters but first we need a head count."

Gary counts the families and finds there are six bedrooms needed plus four beds in the girls and two in the boys dormitories.

"This will work out well. Your rooms will be on the third floor and two families will share a common bath. There is no elevator and the stairs are in the center area."

Bobby and Gary lead the way and each family is placed in a room. They then report to Will, "We have four bedrooms left on the third floor."

Bobby, "We don't know how many of the previously assigned personnel have shown up. I will see how many rooms have names on them and who is missing later."

Will, "Go to your families and get some rest." The families given rooms on the third floor were not known to Will. They were just people seeking a safe shelter.

Will then goes to his room and speaks with his wife Teresa.

"It is going to be rough but we have already taken the first steps and everything is okay so far. Help me figure out how to keep everyone busy so they wont get any further depressed than they are already."

"The most immediate need is to complete the kitchen staff. We have to feed all of these people shortly. The Chef has only three assistances and he is going to need at least ten more....... With Dr. Reeves gone we have no doctor. What are you going to do about that?"

"Jennie has the most medical experience I will put her in charge until Dr Reeves returns and I will find out if anyone else has a medical background."

"If he returns. If he was in Rome when that bomb hit there is no way he could have survived."

"He had only been gone a few minutes when it hit. I pray that he had not gotten far and is able to return. Other immediate needs are for teacher assistances, someone to take care of the plants and the animals. Joe will also need more men on the Security Team because we must remain vigilant twenty-four hours a day."

"Well it looks as though we will have no trouble finding something for everyone to do . I am afraid our worst trouble will stem from the emotional state of being shut up here for an extended time. Maybe we should have a Activities Director to give people something to do in their spare time especially the children."

"To keep morale up, it is essential that everyone be properly fed and that we don't overwork the cooks. I pray the supply of meat doe's not run out before we leave the shelter. Once outside there will no longer be cattle nor any other animals alive to furnish fresh meat. All life not in proper shelters will be dead from radiation or chemical poisoning. Survival of the animals within this shelter is essential to provide meat for future generations."

Will is interrupted by the intercom.

"Dad we have people approaching the front entrance."

Will immediately goes to the control room. Three people are coming one man and two women. The man was carrying one of the girls. As they neared he is recognized as Dr Reeves. Joe opens the outer door and closes it after they entered. He instructs them to remove and dispose of their clothing which they do. He then opened the door to the decontamination room. They entered and go through the process. Joe then opens the door to the dressing room. After dressing in white robes they entered the Hospital. As soon as he knew it was Dr. Reeves, Will had informed his family and they came to greet him. The reunion was a happy one. Leonard's wife had been praying for his safe return, but knew the odds were against it. She then noticed his wounds and started to treat them. Jennie and others put the women in isolation and began to examine them to determine the extent of their injuries. Leonard has second degree burns on his back and is bleeding from his left leg. But appeared to be okay otherwise.

Then Leonard tells what he had experienced.

"I had just started up the hill East of Cave Spring when the explosion occurred. Because of the size of the mushroom cloud there was no doubt it was nuclear. I grabbed the protective suit and jumped into a ditch. I got into the suit just in time. As I lay flat in the ditch, heat from the bomb passed over me. It was so intense it burned my back through the suit. After the wave of heat passed I stood up and looked around. My car was destroyed and it was obvious Rome no longer existed.

I removed the suit and started running back here. All the structures in what had been Cave Spring were in rubble and I saw no signs of Life. Just up the road I came upon the two girls. They had been coming from Alabama and when the turbulence hit their car the driver lost control and they wrecked. I could see they were still alive so I helped them out of the car. I cut my leg doing this. One of them has a broken leg and internal injuries and the other who was still strapped in only suffered cuts and bruises. We then walked here. I didn't thank we would make it. Radiation from the blast has obviously not begun to fall heavily in this area yet."

"The radon count outside is now over 200 when you entered the shelter thirty minutes ago it was 100 and it is rising fast. If it had taken you another hour you would have suffered a fatal dose. You need to rest now. We will talk again later. Stay here in the hospital bed Catherine and Jennie will be here with you and will follow any instructions you give them........ We are all glad you made it back."

Will then goes to the kitchen to see how Jerry was doing with dinner. He was happy to find Teresa there.

"How are they?"

"One girl is seriously injured. The other two are going to be alright. Thank God they made it here. Now what's for dinner I could eat a horse."

"Well it is still an hour before time to eat, so go to our room and get out of our way."

This was her way of telling Will he also needs some rest

Will goes to their room and lays down on the bed. He was restless thinking of the many horrifying things that had happened to his world and to the millions of people who were now dead. It was almost too much to endure and could drive the survivors insane. All of their family and friends not with them were dead and none of them could even be given a funeral or burial. He felt he must remain calm and not show his fears to anyone else. Exhausted he must have dosed off and was awakened by the buzzer signaling dinner in ten minutes.

TERRIBLE EVENTS AND GOOD NEWS
CHAPTER FOUR

As Will washes his face and prepares to go to the dining area, he is running potential problems through his mind and thinking of how to handle them. However; in his wildest thoughts he could not have dreamed of the problem he was about to face.

The buffet is ready with creamed potatoes, cooked carrots, corn, peaches and sirloin steak. Jerry is determined to make everyone's first meal in the shelter a good one. Most of the people had entered the area and serving had began, when two men still dressed in outside clothes come out of the center column. They had hidden pistols in a bag which they had been allowed to bring in and now had the guns in their hands. The gunmen order everyone to move to the left and sit on the floor. As he started to exit his room, Will sees what is happening and steps back inside easing the door closed. Then he hears Joe calling from the Control Room.

"Dad do not leave your room. Two men have guns in the dining area. We are watching um and are at this time working on what action to take. I have unlocked our gun cabinet and have armed Fred, John, and myself with rifles."

"Be prepared but do not act yet as we don't know their intent. I am going to go and talk with them,"

"Wait let me hook you to the intercom system in that area.. You can talk to them from where you are. They don't know our location or they would have come here first."

Will then speaks to the men over the intercom.

"What is the problem? Have we not already saved your lives and now you threaten us with guns. What more do you want?"

"You have imprisoned us and their is no reason for us to stay here. The war is over you told us so yourself."

"Perhaps the war is over but radiation and chemicals left from it are still present outside. To go outside means certain death to anyone who does."

"I don't believe you come out and talk to us to our face."

Will can see these men are ignorant of radiation poisoning and goes out to try and reason with them. He approaches the dining area.

"I am not lying to you. Put away your guns, lets eat and I will explain it to you....... I know now nervous you are. We all feel the same way. No one wants to stay here. We only do so in order to survive."

The second gunman speaks to his accomplice

"Maybe he is right and it is dangerous outside."

"Shut up he's just trying to trick us. I'll tell you what we are going to do. We are going to send him and others outside. If they die we won't go out."

Seeing that Will has their attention, Bobby begins to slowly move people into the kitchen. Teresa and the cooks get in before the men notice what is happening. One fires his gun into the ceiling and says , "I will shoot the next person that moves."

Will tries to assure everyone that everything will soon be okay.

"Please everyone just remain calm and do as they say. It's going to be alright if you do."

The first gunmen orders Bobby, Gary and two others to separate themselves from the group and sends the rest into the kitchen. Everyone does as they are told. He then tells Will and the rest to go to the shelters exit. Joe is watching the procedure and sends two armed guards out of the Control Room with instructions to be as quiet as possible and get into sniper positions. He tells them.

"Do not shoot unless it is absolutely necessary."

At the exit, the renegades order Will to open the door and Will responds to their demand.

"I will do everything you ask but please use me and let the others go."

"You try to delay us one more time and I'm going to shoot you."

Joe is watching the scene unfold by camera when Will speaks to him on the intercom.

"You know how, go ahead and open all of the doors except the last one."

"Go and find where this fellow is opening these doors from and make sure he don't pull any tricks."

The two snipers hear this and step inside the nearest room.

As they enter the dressing room Will speaks to them again.

"Come on go outside with us since you think I am lying." The man thanks about it for a minute and then.

"This is as far as I go now get moving."

Will and the rest walk to the last room. and as they walk he whispers,

"When we get to the last room move to the side fast."

As they jump to the left and right Will yells, "Now" Joe has figured out his dad's plan and already has his hands on the close switches. He throws the switches and all the doors close trapping Will and the others in the first room and the gunman in the third one. As soon as he was sure he had the renegade trapped he opens the door to the decontamination room so Will and the others could decontaminate in case they had been exposed to chemicals. He prayed that the radiation they were exposed to as they had walked toward the exit had not harmed them.

The gunman who had been looking for the Control Room runs back to the exit doors. Joe orders him to drop his gun and walk away from it. The snipers has repositioned themselves and had their sights set on the man. He spots one of them and fires his pistol at him. Both guards fire. This gunman is killed instantly.

The trapped man tries to open the door to the decontamination room using the manual handle, but Joe has overrode this method of opening it. The gunman panics and begins to fire his pistol at the door lock. Diana had been guarding the Control Room door. Joe how sends her down.

The guards position them self outside the doors. The gunman empties his pistol at the lock and Joe opens the doors allowing those in the decontamination and shelter to enter where the man is. Bobby and Gary tackles the man and takes his empty gun. The three guards rush in and John uses the man's belt to tie his hands behind his back. Will then tells his people.

"Lets leave him in this room for now."

Everyone goes into the main shelter and Joe closes the doors trapping the man inside the dressing room. Will instructs John and Fred.

"Take this one to the hospital, let them make sure he is dead and then place him in the crypt . After that stow their weapons and come back here right away. The third guard was Will's niece,

"Are you alright."

She nods, "Yes." and Bobby accompanies her upstairs to stow her weapon.

As they were building the shelter Will had made the decision not to have weapons in it. Joe had talked him into having a small arsenal locked in cabinets in the Control Room. He was now glad he had given in on this. Tonight had proved Joe right.

Gary goes to the hospital to check on his wife Jennie and the rest go toward the kitchen to check on their wives and children. Everyone comes from the kitchen and Will explains what had happened and then asks if anyone knows the gunman. No one did. Gary comes out of the hospital and hears the question.

"These two must have seen others entering and followed everyone inside. I don't think they even knew where they were or why they were here. One of them made a pass at Beverley as we went up the stairs telling her, you can sleep in my room tonight. I told him to watch what he said. She is only fifteen. He didn't answer back so I let it go....... They didn't seem to like it when I assigned them to the dormitory on the third level. One told me they wanted a room on the first level. As he was smiling when he said it, I didn't think much of it."

"Did they have any family with them?"

"No, they were by themselves. This is why I put them in the dormitory."

Bobby comments on what has just occurred.

"What a way to start our new life. I suggest we thank God that we are now safe. Let's have a moment of silence and everyone thank him in their own way." Everyone bows their head. Soon, someone starts the Lord's Prayer and everyone joins in. It was a solemn few minutes and everyone seemed to feel better afterwards.

Teresa then speaks to everyone.

"We must forget the past. What's done is done. Now everyone line up again and lets eat this food while it is still warm. We will all be very active tomorrow."

It was a silent meal but most ate at least a little something.

Joe had scheduled six four hour shifts for the control room and he is now due to be relieved, so Will speaks to Wendell and then to the rest.

"Wendell after you finish eating please go and relieve Joe so he can eat. Too much has happened today. We will have our meeting tomorrow after breakfast."

Gary leaves the table and starts for the serving line.

"I am going to take Jennie and the others in the hospital something to eat."

"Teresa will you and some others help him"

Teresa nodded yes and begins to fix plates of food.

Later, Will goes to the hospital. When his daughter-in law Jennie sees him come in,

"Are you alright. Gary told me what happened."

Will gives her a hug,

"Everyone is okay. Two unknown men just went crazy. One of them is now dead and the other is locked up. How are things here."

"Dr Reeves and Catherine are working with the injured girl he brought in. I x-rayed her and besides a broken leg, she is bleeding internally from several sources. I don't know how she's still alive."

In the operating room, Doctor Reeves is operating on the girl and Catherine is assisting as his nurse. He has the girls body cavity open and is trying to stop the bleeding. Her heart stops and he tries hand massaging it. This doesn't work so he uses the electrical petals. Then goes back to massaging. After a while Catherine speaks to him softly.

"She's gone Leonard. -- You did your best. -- Nobody could have saved her. Her injuries were just to severe."

"If I could have gotten to her sooner."

"Leonard stop it. -- You done your best. -- Now lets close her up and go check talk to her sister."

When Dr Reeves and Catherine come from the operating room. He shakes his head.

"We couldn't save her. I'm going to go and tell her sister."

"Health wise how is the sister and the others in there doing."

"I don't know. I haven't had a chance to check on them as yet."

"Leonard are you okay? What about your leg and back"

"I haven't had time to worry about it."

Doctor Reeves then goes into the isolation room as Teresa, Betty and others enter with food.

Will then heads for the Control Room. Upon entering he hugs Joe.

"Outstanding job son you, Fred and John have just saved some lives. Wendell will be here to relieve you any minute."

"There is too much going on for me to leave. I have been monitoring American aircraft on UHF radio a lot of them have survived and flown South, It seems they are not welcome anywhere. Running low on fuel they have no choice but to land. They are being surrounded by the military and told they will be shot if they attempt to leave their planes."

"Is anyone still in the air."

"Yes."

"Connect me to them.

Will then speaks into the microphone.

"Any aircraft with the US Air Force this is Will Ferguson in a shelter in North Georgia do you read me."

"This is Col. Carter you are coming in loud and clear. We are preparing to land in around ten minutes at Mexico City's Airport the tower has ordered us not to land but we have no choice as fuel is low."

"What is your outfit?"

"The 1st TAC at Langley, Virginia. We were ordered airborne when it was known there was incoming missiles."

Will is happy to hear that some of his old outfit has escaped the devastation.

"I retired from there in 1976 as an Aircraft Maintenance Superintendent. I was one of the original Eagle Keepers. What type aircraft are you flying."

"F-22s....... I flew F-15s in Afghanistan. They are still good birds. The Air National Guard has them now. I hope they got airborne and are heading somewhere South."

"Did any of the ground crews make it out."

"Two C-141s from Shaw were on the base when the evacuation order came. Our crews launched us and some may have been able to get aboard the 141s or other aircraft. I just don't know. How are things where you are?"

"Our shelter has proven itself. The sixty or so here are okay. We are provisioned to stay underground for four years. Besides UHF we are also equipped with short-wave radio, am/fm radio and satellite TV. We are in touch with several shelters. Although all of our known enemies have been destroyed the United States no longer exist as a nation. I suggest you try and make friends when you land because the air here is poisoned and the radiation count is over 500 radon's per hour. To go outside here would mean certain death. Please contact us when you can and we will let you know when it is safe to come home. Our call sign is Phoenix."

"We are landing now. It has lifted our spirits talking to you, pray for us."

"May God be with you......out."

Joe then gives his dad more good news.

"I have been talking to some U.S. Navy ships by short-wave most of them are heading for Australia the rest are trying to make it to South Africa or South America. They have suffered heavy losses and are limping South."

"At least many are still alive and those going to Australia or South America will find a safe port. The others, I'm afraid still have some fighting to do. Try and contact the USS Missouri your cousin Robert is aboard it."

"Phoenix calling USS Missouri come in please."

After several attempts he is answered,

"This is the Missouri. Who am I talking with."

"Joe Ferguson from a shelter in North Georgia. Do you have a Doctor Robert Munoz on board? His parents are here and want to know if he is safe."

"We have a lot injured. I will check. Remain on this frequency and I will call you back."

Will is elated at the happenings. Thousands of American were still alive

"Put me on the full intercom. --- We are in touch with our Air Force and Navy. The aircraft are landing in Mexico City and the Navy is sailing toward Australia and other points South. Some of our military has survived. --- Munoz family report to the Control Room. --- Joe have any other shelters contacted us yet?"

"Not yet I'll try to contact them soon."

Wendell enters with their food for the Control Room Crew and Will tells Joe.

"Come on son eat and let Wendell start trying to contact them."

Just then Shelter two reports in.

"This is Henry. We have had a problem but dealt with it. Three are dead and two wounded including myself."

"What happened?"

"A man came to the entrance and when we got him to medical I looked at him. It was apparent he had suffered a fatal dose of radiation. He was burned over his entire body. I tried to give him an injection for the pain and he went crazy. A security guard was standing next to the gurney. This fellow grabbed the guards gun and began shooting everyone in sight. Another guard heard the shooting, came in and shot the man but not before he had killed three and wounded the nurse and me."

"How bad are the wounds,"

"Gloria was hit in the left shoulder. I was lucky the bullet grazed my head knocking me out for a while."

"We have also had problems. We have one dead and one prisoner. Dr. Reeves is injured but functioning. Was the man decontaminated as he entered?"

"Yes, and we have placed his body in the crept."

"Joe and I will suit up and see what can be done in the passageway. If possible we will get through and bring you and the nurse here for treatment. Lay down and rest until we get there."

Just then Will's Brother-in-law Johnny, his wife Linda and the rest of the Munoz family come rushing in. Will tells them as he starts to leave.

"Joe and I have an emergency. We have to go. Wendell has some possible good news for you. --- Come on Joe."

As they go toward the passageway, Gary and Bobby sees them, "What's going on?" Will, "We are going to try and get through to the other shelter they need help." Gary, "Lets go." The four of them go into the dressing room attached to the tunnel, don protective suits and remove radiation and chemical detectors from their cabinets. Will calls the Control Room.

"Wendell open the tunnel doors and close them as soon as we get clear. Also monitor our movements in the passageway."

The passageway has caved in about fifty feet from the shelter. They survey the damage and find three main beams have given way on the right side allowing dirt and small rock to block the tunnel. Will sees if they tried to open the entire passageway more debris would come down upon them. He decides to attempt and shore up the fallen beams before digging. Gary, Bobby and Joe had been checking for radiation and other contaminants as Will checked the cave in. Only normal amounts were found so they removed their protective suits.

Will was now glad he had decided to store the I-beams that were left over from constructing the shelters at each end of the tunnel. House jacks and shovels were also stored there. He contacts Wendell,

"Send us more help. We have to prop up these beams."

There is no reason for them to wear protective suits as the air is good here. Contact Shelter Two and have them send in several men. Tell them to bring a house jack, shovels, one long and several short I-beams to the fallen in area."

The equipment is brought forth and Will instructs a man from either side to begin digging toward each other as high as possible and a shovel's length from the West wall.

"I want a hole from one side to the other large enough for an I-beam to pass through."

The digging goes well and within the hour the diggers have broken through to each other but dirt is refilling the hole. Will orders.

"Hurry push the large I-beam through to the other side Before it fills up." This accomplished he then tells them to turn a short beam sideways on top of the jacks and use them to raise the long beam. The procedure seems to be working but as the beams are lifted more rocks and dirt pour into the tunnel.

"Stop, the broken beams are not going back into place. Leave the jacks as they are and we might be able to clear a way next to the West wall." They began digging slowly next to the wall. It takes a few hours but a four foot wide path is cleared through to the other side.

Not sure how long the opening would last. Will has steel plates brought forth and placed against the dirt then braced them with four feet I-beams. He now thanks the volunteers and tells them to return to their families. Bobby, Gary, Joe and Will go through the opening to Shelter Two. Henry had given Glenda another pain killer and had a compression pact on her shoulder to help control the bleeding. They use gurneys to transport her and Henry to the hospital in Shelter One.

Dr. Reeves had finished the examinations on the ladies in

isolation. He gave Joyce and Cynthia antibiotics as they only had slight colds and sent them to their families. Brenda is lucky to be alive after the car crash but x-rays show no major damage. She was just bruised and sore. Leonard decides to keep her overnight for observation. Teresa, Shirley and Betty are also at the hospital. They are waiting for Will and the boys to return.

When the injured nurse is brought in, Catherine has redressing Leonard's leg wound and was treating the burns on his back. Jennie hooked up an IV to Glenda and takes her into x-ray to determine the extent of her injury.

The nurse was lucky the bullet didn't hit any vital organs but was lodged in the back of her shoulder. It had gone almost all the way through her. Dr. Reeves examined Henry and determines he had a concussion. He has Betty show Henry a hospital bed and tells him to rest until tomorrow. Leonard and Catherine then prepared to operate on Glenda and remove the bullet. Betty and Shirley volunteer to watch over the patients till morning. Will then looks at Leonard and Catherine."

"Leonard, as soon as you can, get some rest. Catherine, make him go to your room as soon as you finish with Brenda."

Joe, Gary, Bobby, Teresa and Will leave to see what had happened in the Control Room. Outside the hospital everyone was hanging around wanting to know what all had happened. Gary speaks to the people.

"Everything is alright. You can go and relax anytime you wish. You will be okay now. Remember the breakfast buzzer sounds at 0750hrs. We will give you a report over the intercom if anything else happens tonight."

In the Control room, the Munoz family is ecstatic. They had talked to Robert over the radio for almost two hours. He was okay and had told them his ship was heading to Australia. He was very happy to hear that his family was safe. He had sent his wife Jessica and daughter Nathalie to San Antonio before he boarded ship and this was the first time he had heard from them since. The Munoz's were too excited to go to there rooms and had stayed with Wendell.

Joe speaks to Freddy and John, who were the guards that had shot the gunman.

"You did a great job today. Thanks for helping save Dad's and other peoples lives. Freddy it is 0300hrs now will you relieve me at 0800 and John will you relieve him at 1200hrs."

Diana who had been with her children comes in and Joe looks at her.

"Diana will you relieve John at 1400hrs."

They all nod yes and Joe continues.

"Tomorrow we will recruit more people to help. There will be six four hour shifts daily and you three will be in charge of three of them. Wendell you will head the shift relieving Diana at 1800hrs. Now why don't you go with your families and get some rest."

They start to leave the room and Linda tells her husband.

"Come on Johnny lets go."

"You go ahead. I'm going to stay here for a while." Wendell responds to this.

"Good I have picked up several transmissions in Spanish and can't understand a word they say."

Wendell then reports to Will.

"So far, I have been able to contact twenty-one other shelters. The shelters all held good but most of them had troubles with panicking or from outsiders they had let in. Sounds familiar doesn't it. All of the other call signs are here. Gary do you want to try for a while?"

"I might as well as Bobby and I are going to stay here with Joe tonight. Let me talk to Jennie first and tell her,"

Only a few were still lingering around when Teresa and Will leave the Control Room. They go by the hospital to see how everything was going and are happy to find Leonard and Catherine have left for the night. Betty comments on Leonard.

"Dr. Reeves is so tired he could hardly walk. He said tomorrow he will need a volunteer to give blood for Glenda. Her blood type is O-positive so there should be no trouble finding that. He gave Glenda, Henry and Gloria something to help them sleep and left me some morphine in case they need it later."

Everyone had left the lobby as Will and Teresa are finely able to head for their room. They are exhausted and within minutes of going to bed both are asleep snuggled close together. Tomorrow would truly be another day and no one knows what it might bring.

A BAD DAY IN THE SHELTER
CHAPTER FIVE

It seemed as though their heads had just touched the pillow when the 0750 buzzer sounded. Although both desired to just stay in bed, they knew duty was calling. Teresa and Will get ready and go to the dining area. . Many decisions must be made today.

Anxiety had caused most everyone a restless night. The area was already full of people just milling around. Jerry had the buffet ready but no one was eating as of yet. Teresa gets the meal underway.

"Come on everybody don't let this food go to waste."

People then file through, gather their food and begin to eat. After breakfast Will addresses the people.

"We have several orders of business that must be faced. First what to do about our prisoner. As this is a true Democracy. The adults here are the jury. There is no time to deliberate. Each of you know the facts. Write down either keep him locked up or send him outside. Your votes will then be read aloud and the opinion with the most votes will prevail."

Teresa passes out pencils and paper.

"Vote your true feelings and please do not sign your name."

The room is very quiet as everyone votes and then passes the papers forward where Joyce collects them. Will then asks for assistances.

"I need three volunteers to record the votes as they are

read. As three men come forward, Will points at a man sitting near him.

"Would you please read each vote for the recorders."

As all in attendance listens, the votes are read.

"Recorders compare your count to insure each recorded the same numbers and then report to the group."

The votes went six to keep him locked up as a prisoner and the rest were for sending him outside. This worried Will but he would respect the majority's vote. This man had after all been willing to kill others. Will then sends the condemned man his last meal.

"Diana choose three strong men and take this pitiful individual a meal. Be careful there is no telling how he may react."

Jerry fixes a nice plate of ham, eggs, grits, toast and coffee, places it on a tray and hands it to Diana. When the doors are opened the renegade is sitting in a corner. He had gotten free from his belt restraint and was clutching his bag. As Diana nears him she sees he has been playing with the bags contents. It was full of money. He looked at her.

"What you want?"

Diana sits the tray down and leaves. She tells the group what she had seen and what she thinks of the him.

"They must have robbed someone and were looking for a place to hide when they came here. He's a thief."

Will then schedules the days priorities.

"We will wait until later to deal with him as more pressing matters are before us. First we must bury the girl that died last night and we must also bury the other renegade."

It comes to Will that perhaps some have not heard about the dead girl. He tells how Dr. Reeves had rescued this young girl and her sister Ann and that she had died from her injuries. Then.

"Is there a preacher with us." Billy holds up his hand.

"The assembly area is now among other things your new church. Will you conduct the ceremonies?"

Billy nods, "Yes." and Teresa asks.

"Jennie will you bring the gurney on which the girl lays to the assembly area."

The body is rolled into the area and Billy begins the service.

"What is her name?"

Ann answers "Jean." Billy then leads his new congregation in prayer for Jean's soul. After the service, Jean's body is taken to the crypt. As several watch, her body is placed in a vault and the opening is sealed. Will decides to wait until later to bury the renegade in respect for the girl they had just interned.

After the ceremonies all the adults volunteer for the various task needing coverage. At this time everyone is asked to list their family on a roster so the number of people in the shelter would be known. This is necessary to insure the correct amount of food could be prepared at each meal to avoid waste. They discover only sixty-one are now in the shelter, eighteen couples, twelve children and thirteen others.

The plumber and his family were among those who had not made it to the shelter. Bobby and Gary would have to work together as electricians, mechanical technicians, security and now plumber. All thought it sad that only a little over half of the shelters capacity was filled. Will once again addresses the residents.

"Until we get to know each others name. I suggest we all wear nametags. I have noticed most are already wearing one. The others will find some on the table up front here. ---- I would appreciate it if we could call each other by our first names as we are to be as one family for a while."

By now it is lunch time and Jerry suggests everyone eat and before going about their various task. Will and Teresa sit and talk with the Dentist Bill Jones and his wife Dora.

"I see Dora is your assistant. This is good."

"We are going to schedule everyone for a checkup. We must try to prevent problems before they occur because of our limited supplies." Teresa talks of her job.

"Two have volunteered to help me with the general store. Now that we have everyone's name we are going to make rations sheets for each person. I will also type the list and make copies for whom ever needs them."

After lunch everyone goes their various ways and Will discusses the kitchen with Jerry.

"Did you get enough volunteers?"

"Yes and most have restaurants experience. I have already scheduled six to prepare breakfast and lunch and another six for dinner. I will work with both shifts at least until I am sure of their skills."

"Good and be sure to give the Dentist a list of those on each shift so he can schedule checkups that will not interfere with their kitchen duties."

"Okay."

Will then makes his way to the hospital. Leonard, Catherine and Jennie have relieved Betty and brought food for the patients. As Will enters he comments.

"Some day yesterday uh?"

Leonard smiles, "I hope I never see another one like it. I am still worn out from it."

" Have you had a chance to check on your patients yet?"

"I was just going to do that."

Will waits as the Doctor makes his checks. Henry was the first to come from the room.

"I hope you feel better than you look."

Henry answers without responding to Will's attempt at humor.

"Like I was run over by a Mack truck. Dr. Reeves said I would be okay in a couple of days."

"You were lucky." Henry nods "Yeah." as Leonard re-enters the room.,

"Glenda is going to be alright but she has lost a lot blood and could use a transfusion. Catherine is redressing her wound."

Will speaks to the control room and ask them to make an announcement asking for volunteers to donate type O positive blood.

Judy enters the room.

"I am a Medical Lab Technician. Bobby sent me here can you use me?"

"I'll say we can. Come on in. There is an unmanned fully equipped lab upstairs. It is now yours."

Will then asks Leonard, "After Glenda recovers can you use her here."

"I sure can. we would then be fully staffed and have a nurse on duty at night."

"We will do this then but she will still quarter in Shelter One, at least for a while."

Satisfied that things are improving in the hospital. Will then goes to the control room. Fred is on duty along with Ed and Norm.

"What's happened since I was last here?"

"A lot but first look at the prisoner. He has been just sitting there holding that bag all day. He didn't eat his breakfast and hasn't even looked at his lunch. I thank he has gone mad."

"Open the doors behind him to the outside."

As soon as the doors are open, the man jumps up and runs outside while continuing to tightly grip his bag. He apparently had lost his mind. The doors are closed and they watch the renegade by camera until he disappears into the dust cloud.

Fred watches the man go and then gives Will a report.

"Thank god none of us had to put him out there. --- Other shelters have been calling all morning. People are scared. They are apparently just realizing what has happened. Most didn't believe the war would come to the total destruction of their way of life."

"Have your men contact everyone they can and speak to whomever is in charge. Tell them the only way to settle their occupants down is to follow their shelter plan and give everyone something to do, keep them busy and stress they have survived. If you can, get the number of people in each shelter. I would like to know America's new population count. --- Have you been in contact with anyone other than the shelters?"

"Yes, we have talked to people in several South American countries. They seem to be amazed that we are still alive. Brazil has sent reconnaissance drones over what was the United States. They say every major city has been destroyed and no active life was spotted."

"I pray thousands are safe within shelters in areas other than our own. Fred be sure to keep accurate records of everyone you talk to."

Just then Shelter Two radios with trouble.

"We need help. A man has been stirring up the people. We are about to have a riot on our hands. He is demanding we open the outside doors. --- Wait they are on the move. It looks as thought they are going to try and take over the Control Room."

"What is your name and how many are with you? Shelter two, "I am George and there are two others in here."

"Lock the door and arm yourselves. Do not let them inside lives depend on it. Help is on the way."

Will turns to Fred.

"Unlock the weapons cabinet and notify all security to report to the passageway doors. Ed, Norm, bring several weapons and follow me."

Joe, Gary, Bobby, John, Diana and others arrive at the tunnel doors. As the doors are opening, Henry comes out of the hospital.

"What's going on?"

"Grab a nightstick and come on."

As they arrive at Shelter Two they hear a scuffle upstairs and gunfire. The rioters have broken into the Control Room and those inside have fired shots into the floor in an attempt to stop them.

Joe yells commands.

"Up the stairs quick. Use your flashlights or nightsticks to put them down. Don't shoot unless necessary."

The rioters have almost taken over when Joe and the others arrive. They are beating George and the others. The security force rushes in, subdues and handcuffs the troublemakers. Will then speaks to his son.

"Joe take them into the crept and lock um in. Leave the handcuffs on them for now. Then take everyone back to the other shelter."

Will turns to Henry, "Can you handle it from here?"

"Yes, I had not had a chance to get fully organized before I was shot. I see a strong loyal force is a necessity and George and I will get this taken care of."

"Be sure to talk to everyone about how important staying inside is. Everyone voted on what to do with our renegade and I suggest you do the same here. This seemed to unite those in out shelter as they now knew their opinion counts. Good luck and keep us posted."

Will goes back to the hospital. Catherine was redressing Leonard's leg.

"Leonard you have done more than your share, why don't you go to bed and rest. Catherine and Jennie will call you if needed."

"I thank I will. By the way, we drew blood from six people. Glenda got her transfusion and we have a supply of whole blood on hand."

It is now time to bury the renegades corpse before it starts to smell. John had just relieved Fred and Will had him announce the burial over the intercom. The man had been put in a body bag and with little fanfare is placed in the vault on the far end of the crept. As far as possible from the girls body. Billy has a brief service for the man.

"It's sad, he died for a bag of worthless money. Everyone join me in praying that those now in the shelter will survive and no other body will have to be interned here."

Suddenly, John called from the Control Room.

"Will I have a Colonel Carter on short wave and he is asking to speak to you."

Will rushes upstairs to the Control Room and John opens the intercom so everyone could hear.

"Colonel good to hear from you. What's your status?"

"The Mexicans thought we were invading them. Our Ambassador convinced them otherwise. I thought you would like to know, most of our ground crews were on the 141's and are now safe."

"Where are all of you staying?"

"We are all at the American Embassy. I made a deal with the Mexican Government, traded two aircraft for a bag of Paso's and service to the rest of our aircraft. The Airborne Command Center has also landed here. The Vice President is safe.

"Have you heard from anyone else, in the United States?"

"We are trying but so far you are the only one answering."

"Most of the shelters in our area are okay but are having radio problems."

"We will try to contact you daily at 1400hrs your time."

"Good we will exchange information then. -- Out."

The dinner buzzer sounds and everyone gathers. They are for the first time talking and even smiling among themselves. Shirley, Bonnie and Edna had attended to the fish, chickens and rabbits. Johnny and Linda had watered and cared for the plants. Each of the others had been busy at their task.

Will had decided earlier not to turn on the television in the lobby for this day, out of respect for the burials and to give the people a chance to recover before seeing and hearing more bad news. After dinner he speaks to his Granddaughters Kamilah.

"Go to the library and pick four movies for this evening. Bring comedies with a happy ending."

Will knows only one can be shown but he will let others decide which one.

As he watches the movie Will thinks, "It's amazing how much everyone has been through in the last two days and most are now laughing at a movie." He can not help but wonder what tomorrow would bring. Could everything settle into a routine or will all hell break out again.

DAY THREE BAD, BUT IMPROVES
CHAPTER SIX

The third morning, Joe is relieved. He comes and joins his parents for breakfast.

"Son how did it go last night?"

"I didn't wake you as there was really nothing we could do about it. We have lost contact with at least ten of the shelters. Others are having trouble of one kind or another. I logged it all in and it would be best if you read the log."

"Okay. I am going by the hospital and then I will read it."

"When you are ready let me know and I'll go to the Control Room with you."

Fred turns on the television in the main lobby and hospital area. It is tuned to a station in Mexico City. Several people are watching and hoping for some favorable news. Johnny is interpreting the Spanish for them.

"Northern Mexico near the United States border has a deadly radioactivity count of over 400 radon's per hour. Those that could be were evacuated further South. Mexico City has a tremendous influx of refugees with over a million of them coming from the United States. All are hungry and many are sick from radiation poisoning. All hospitals are filled to capacity and there is no place for the rest to go. The American dollar and credit cards are now worthless so the hotels are not accepting anyone trying to use them. There is no longer a World Relief Organization and the Mexican Government is trying to deal with the problem. - Individual families are taking in as many as they can."

At the hospital, Glenda is on her feet and anxious to return to Shelter Two. Leonard tells her,

"Not yet, stay here for at least two more days. We must be more careful now than ever before. We only have a limited supply of antibiotics and I want to insure no infection sets in."

Will enters at this time.

"How is your leg Leonard?" Catherine answers, "He needs to stay off it for a few of days. It took ten stitches to close the wound and he has been on it continuously."

"Leonard you heard your better half and I agree with her. At this time, you are more of a health risk than anyone else."

"Okay you two, you win. I will just relax and see how it goes."

Besides the station from Mexico, Fred, Carlos and Sam are monitoring television stations from Northern Canada, Greenland, Australia and South Africa. Will is glad that more people have survived the war than had been predicted. Perhaps many more were also safe somewhere in the United States. Joe begins searching for more satellite televisions stations when a station from Fairbanks Alaska suddenly comes in.

"This is Channel 11 in Fairbanks Alaska we have been off the air and in a shelter. The radon count here has not as yet reached a critical point. It is however high enough that no one is outside for more than thirty minutes at a time. We are setting up a short wave radio and it will be operational by tomorrow. Our call sign will be Mt. McKinley. If anyone is out there please contact us."

This is good news and Fred announces the contact to everyone over the intercom.

"Thank God for satellites. Maybe, other stations will come back on the air. Keep searching and keep each station you find on a different screen, even is you have to shut off some outside cameras, and be sure to log everything that happens."

Will sits down and begins to read the log entries from the night before. Of the shelters previously contacted, only fourteen were still answering and twelve of them were reporting some type trouble. Shelter fourteen had electrical problems and had been advised to switch to their fuel cell generators. They reported because of the large amount of fuel stored for the gas generators they had decided not to purchase other backup generators. Their fuel tanks had exploded from the heat when a nuclear bomb struck downtown Atlanta. They were operating off of battery power only. Joe had looked up their location. They were outside of Kennesaw just thirty miles from downtown Atlanta. The following conversation was recorded in the log.

Joe, "How many are in your shelter? Shelter, answer, "Forty-two." "Do you have that many protective suits?" Answer, "Yes." Joe, "How much breathing oxygen do you have in your medical area?" Answer, "Four bottles." Joe, "I suggest you stay where you are until the air starts to go bad then don your protective suits and try to make it to Shelter thirteen. You should have a map with your survival book showing its location. The longer you can wait the better chance you will have." Carlos, "As long as the plants stay alive you will have oxygen. If your baby chickens begin to die it is time to leave." Shelter, "We didn't bring any animals inside." Shaking his head. Joe, "Good luck try to keep us informed."

Will is discussed and can read no more.

"I spent weeks figuring exactly what provisions each shelter must have and writing an Instruction Book on how to survive. They chose to ignore this in order to save some now useless money. I hope it doesn't cost them their lives and I wonder if others followed their example. I certainly hope not.-- Joe instruct all your personnel, tell everyone they talk to, the only way to survive is to follow their Instruction Book to the letter."

John and his crew enter and relieve Fred, Carlos and Diana. Diana is ready to go.

"Hey you guys, its lunch time. Come on Carlos lets eat."

Fred briefs John and then follows the others toward the dining area. Will talks to John.

"Have you all eaten." John, "Yes." "Let me know if anything sufficient happens."

He then leaves to find Teresa and have her join him for lunch.

At 1400, Will is back in the Control Room awaiting communications from Col. Carter in Mexico City. Right on time.

"Phoenix this is American Embassy in Mexico City."

"Come in Embassy."

"This is Col. Carter it is a nightmare here. Thousands of refugees are trying to come into the compound. Our C-141's have began transporting people to Australia but the military is having trouble maintaining order and this is slowing things.

The Vice President has been in touch with some American ships docked at Acapulco. He is trying to arrange transportation for the refugees to get there. Over."

"We understand your dilemma. We are receiving television from there and they say over one-million Americans refugees are without food or shelter. We have lost contact with several shelters in our area and don't know their static. Over."

"The Ambassador has made contact with Hawaii. No missiles hit there and so far they are okay. Also Guam has reported no problems so far. With some exceptions like Russia, most who live below the 20th parallel and above the 60th are okay. The Middle East, China, Africa, Europe and the United States took the blunt of the nuclear and chemical weapons. We will keep you abreast of events daily. Over and out."

John had put the conversation with the embassy on the intercom so all could hear. Will then tells John.

"We are hearing of more and more people who are okay and I figure each day will put us in contact with even more. Contact as many other shelters as you can and exchange news with them. Dwell on the good things and skip the bad. The other shelters have enough to worry about."

Will had decided to transmit only good news. If they had installed it, most shelters had the same communication capabilities as Shelter One and were also searching short wave radio frequencies.

"Even though mainland America was hit hard, part of

Alaska, Hawaii, Puerto Rico and other areas are okay so far. It remains to be seen how far the radiation will spread."

John orders his crew.

"Close the lens covers on all outside cameras. There is so much dust in the air it has been pitch dark for the last twenty-four hours and we can't see anything anyway. We must pray for rain. Without rain to settle the dust it will be that way for a long time. With good rains we could be going outside in a couple of years."

Will decides to walk around and talk to people who were involved with their daily tasks. Linda sees him coming.

"Have you talked with Robert?"

"Not this morning. Being a doctor, I'm sure he has little time with so many injured to care for."

Johnny tells his wife.

"That's right Linda. He is all right so don't worry about him. He'll be okay."

Kamilah had volunteered to become the Activities Director. She organizes basketball teams, exercise classes, chess tournaments, arts and crafts sessions and in time sports competition between Shelter one and Shelter Two. The shelter is also equipped with computers on which games are played and a well stocked library. Will was glad the shelter was able to support these activities especially basketball even though it was on a small scale. These activities gave people something to think about other than their predicament of being prisoners to the outside poisons.

As days and then months pass nature began to take its course and the single men and women begin to pair off. Joe and Ann are the first couple to be attracted to each other. They attend the evening movies and with each passing day find more reasons to be together. Soon they are feeling the pressures of living under strict shelter rules and want to become more intimate with each other. They begin to visit the shelters top operations room on the pretends of using the periscope to view the outside world. Of course, it is dark outside and the periscope is useless but this gives them the excuse they need in order to be alone. The operations room is crammed with supplies which furnishes a place where their love blossoms and grows.

Soon others pair off Freddy, Jr. found Mary's charm irresistible and they also wish to be alone. By the end of the first six months Milton is the only man unattached. One day he approaches Will.

"Are there any unattached women in Shelter Two?"

"When you are off shift why don't you go over there and see."

Milton made regular trips to Shelter Two after that.

All of this young love about them, brings back memories to the married couples. It seems only yesterday that they too were moon struck. It also helps them look forward to daily returning to the privacy of their room. Indeed without the pressures they had lived with before the war, love as it was when they first met returns to them.

Billy is asked if marriage was possible and one even asked

if it was necessary. Billy tells them to let him see what he could do about it. He then goes to Will.

"People want to get married. What can I do?"

"I thank this is great. When do they want this to happen?"

"I don't know yet. But by whose authority, can I perform a ceremony?"

"That is the easiest question I've had to answer in a while, by the highest authority of all, God's. Are you not one of his spokesman?. --- Keep me informed."

Not long after Billy goes to the Control Room and says he wants to make an announcement. The intercom is opened and a mike is handed to him.

"I have been in conference with six couples from this shelter and two from Shelter Two who wish to get married. They have asked if they could all be wed in one ceremony June 15th, at 1400hrs. I told them yes."

Applause could be heard from throughout the shelters. Will then makes an announcement.

"All potential grooms report to the General Store ASAP."

Everyone wonders what this is about and many follow the grooms to the store. At the store.

"Those of you not getting married will have to wait until later to learn the secret. Grooms go inside."

When they are inside Teresa closes the door.

"Men this is a big step you are about to take and none of you want to do it without listening to what Teresa has to say."

All eyes immediately turn to Teresa.

"No woman wants to get married without rings."

She then holds out a box filled with smaller boxes.

"Come and take a set. It doesn't matter which box you take as they are all the same."

Everyone is all smiles as the boxes are opened to reveal a set of wedding rings.

"Now go to your woman and don't tell a sole until you are alone with her and ask her again to be your bride."

As the men rush out and pass those waiting outside, they were truly happy but none spoke, as to why. Will hugs his wife.

"Well darling you were right again. Its a good thing you did bringing those rings inside with you. They embraced and recalled together the time when he had went to his knees and asked for her hand some fifty-three years ago.

The women form a committee and together with the future brides begin to make plans for the weddings. They told no one of their plans but assure everyone it would be a grand affair. The shelter would be abuzz with gossip of the coming event until June 15th.

The day finely arrives and the speculation and anxiety over what was to happen was almost overbearing to some. Will declares it a holiday and except for the kitchen staff everyone was off. Several others volunteer to help in the kitchen. Will even asks Joe to close the Control Room for the day and Henry to bring everyone from Shelter One to the event. The crowd begins to gather around 1330 and by 1350hrs. have settled into their seats.

The grooms dressed in their outside clothes are all nervously pacing back and forth when over the intercom the song 'Here Comes The Bride" is played and out of the nearest bedroom comes the six brides. Each accompanied by her father or father stand-in. Many could not believe their eyes, the brides are all dressed in beautiful bridal gowns. This was the big secret the wedding Committee had kept from everyone. They had taken white robes and fashioned them into gowns with flowing trains and lace to adorn them. They also wore lace facial veils. It was enough to ensure everyone that life would carry on no matter the obstacles that must be faced. The ceremony is normal except where the preacher does not say by the authority of some governing agency. He simply stated by the authority granted to me by God.

After the weddings Jerry makes an announcement.

"It is time for the reception to begin."

This is also a surprise as only those working on the dinner knew of it. The newly married couples follow Jerry to the dining area. The brides begin to cry as not only is a fine meal prepared but there are six wedding cakes on the table to the left. Many had also fashioned wedding gifts in the craft classes. Several toast are given. Afterwards dinner music is played and the dancing lasts late into the night. It had truly been a day to remember not only for the Brides and Grooms but for all who were there.

The weddings were the morale booster needed to insure everyone they were going to be alright. Life underground becomes accepted as almost a normal thing. The day to day pressures previously experienced are gone. With no business worries, no bills to pay, only a little work and plenty of activities in which to participate most become content with their new lives. The problems married couples had faced no longer exist and the strong love they knew when first wed returns. The shelter becomes almost a utopia. Each day was awaited with anticipation of what would happen next.

After this much joy, what would the future bring to once again lower their spirits?

AN UNEXPECTED SURPRISE
CHAPTER SEVEN

News from the Control Room continues to be favorable as it becomes known that more and more areas have survived. In the fall as the winds changes to the North, the radiation intensity begins to slowly decrease near the 60th. parallel. Will cautions the Control Room crews not to over emphasize this when announcing the daily news to Shelters One and Two.

"This is good news but remember we are much further South and it will take longer to clear here."

It had been over a year and the outside was still under a nuclear winter. Once daily an outside camera and flood lights were activated to check the surroundings area. Through the year 2011 the air had remained full of dust. Then in January of 2012, Joe calls for Will to come to the Control Room.

"Dad look outside."

Will viewed what he felt was a beautiful sight, it was hailing. The dust was coming down as mud but it was coming down.

"This is great but once again, remember it will still take a good while before the radiation is down to a safe level. Announce the hail to everyone and tell them we predict the Spring rains will help clear the air enough that we can see the area by sunlight. As soon as this occurs, we'll show what the camera's see on the big screen in the lobby."

Slowly as hail, snow or rain fell in the area the dust settles and by the end of December the area can be viewed without artificial light. Nothing is alive outside no vegetation is growing, no birds are flying and an eerie silent stillness is everywhere.

A feeling of despair began to fill the minds of those inside. The thought of returning to the outside world and its problems had been put aside and now it appeared this could happen.

The kitchen had been out of fresh fruit and potatoes for over a year and is low on its supply of frozen meats. Their stock of rice, flour, corn meal and beans are at the half way point. All meals will soon be prepared from cans. This too is of limited supply. Jerry reasoned that unless the kitchen was restocked he would have to begin rationing food by mid 2013.

Shelter Two personnel move their remaining food supplies to Shelter One and most meals are now eaten there. They also spent a lot of time in the larger shelter. As this area was designed for one-hundred people this is no problem. They sleep in Shelter Two and come over to Shelter One around noon daily after completing their tasks.

Will discusses the food supplies with Jerry.

"Jerry you have kept the rabbit, fish and chicken population under control by dressing out the extra ones. How much of this meat do you now have stored?"

"I have used fresh meat each time there was enough for a meal, so not much."

"It is imperative that we keep breeding stock alive as they may be our only source of meat when we go outside."

"I know. I have been feeding them table scraps from the beginning so the ladies have not had to use much of the stored dry feed for this."

"That's good, keep up the good work."

In April of 2013, Will makes an announcement.

"The outside radiation readings have been slowly dropping for over a year now and the gas chlomatographs do not register any chemical poisoning agents in the area. As soon as the radon count drops below fifty per hour, we will send a recon party in search of supplies. We are stocked for at least another year before it becomes a serious problem. We have conquered all our problems by working together as a family and if we remain this way everything will be alright."

In September, a recon party of two is formed. Dressed in decontamination suits with camera's mounted in the helmets and riding ATVs, they head toward Cave Spring. Will and others monitor their progress from the Control Room.

"Shelter this is Recon." Shelter, "Go ahead."

"Are you receiving our video? We are about to enter what was Cave Spring. As you see, only rubble is left. We will checkout the remains of the Quick Shop first."

"Joe, what is the radon count there?" Joe, "Near fifty."

"You have thirty minutes. Give the town a fast check and rush back here." "Okay dad."

After returning to the shelter Joe reports.

"There were corpse all over but no signs of life. The grocery store's walls were still standing and we brought back some cans for testing. After we decontaminated, I checked a can of peaches and it appears to be okay."

"Take your samples to the lab and let Gloria confirm your readings."

Gloria found the decontamination process had cleaned the cans and the food inside them was eatable. When Will announces this, a cheer can be heard coming from all areas.

"Now that we know food is available for us to restock, everything is working out for us. We will wait for a few more good rains to lower the radiation even more and then bring in the supplies. Joe notify the other shelters of your findings and ask if they have sent out a recon."

"Only six of the others are still reporting in. The rest decided to go outside weeks ago. I don't know their faith."

"How sad and they were so close to making it through."

Will sits down and reviews the log entries over the past two years. Mexico City had been evacuated because the radiation covering the United States was moving South. Millions had fled toward South America. Col. Carter had radioed all United States aircraft and personnel there were going to attempt to evacuate to Hawaii. He had later reported that most did not make it because of the throng of people trying to board the aircraft. Only the Airborne Control Room with the Vice President, one C-141 and six of the F-22's had gotten airborne. None of the ground crews had made it. Most had given their lives holding back the panic-stricken people as others launched the aircraft that did escape.

In 2012, the 1st. TAC had flown recon missions over

China. The Chinese had arranged shelters for millions of their people inside mountains, but apparently had not stored sufficient supplies and those who had survived the war were forced outside to forage for food. This of course caused their death, from radiation poisoning. The recon pilots reported bodies scattered throughout the country and no life visible anywhere. Their Military and government had been destroyed. Recon missions over the Middle East and other areas also confirmed the same conditions there. The worlds population had been significantly reduced.

Life on the mainland forty-eight states no longer existed except for the few people who were still in properly built shelters. And each of these was still in danger. The builders of many shelters had saved money by modifying the construction of their shelters plans, not fully equipping them or not storing sufficient supplies. They had saved their now worthless money but had given their lives to do it.

There is very little good news in the log. The best is that part of Alaska, Hawaii, and U.S. territorial islands in the Pacific Ocean had survived the war with minimal causalities. The Vice President was attempting to re-establish the National Government from the remnants of what had been the mightiest nation in the world.

The Control Room had kept in touch with others throughout the remaining countries of the world. All were affected one way or another. International trade was at a standstill. Refugees swarming into Central and South America was destroying these nations economy. Brazil had placed its army along its Northern border with orders to kill anyone attempting to enter. Their border was amassed with the bodies of those seeking refuge.

Will has read all the bad news he wish when Joe called to him.

"Dad listen to this."

From the short wave radio comes a familiar voice from the past.

"Can anyone hear me. Is anyone out there? This is the President of the United States. The rubble has been removed allowing a passage out. The radiation is still bad outside but our radio has been repaired. Does anyone out there hear me?"

"Mister President this is Phoenix a shelter in North Georgia. It is good to hear your voice."

"Phoenix thank god others are still alive out there. You are the only one we have reached so far. Have you been in touch with others?"

"Yes sir, there are about four hundred in shelters in our area. Most of the Navy and part of the Air Force are still in tact. The Vice-President and his Staff are in Hawaii which was not hit during the war. Northern Alaska and a few other areas are alright. Most nations between the 20th and 60th parallel no longer exist. Those who caused this disaster no longer exist.

"May God forgive us all."

It was obvious from his voice that the president was crying. Another voice then comes on and asks.

"Will you give us the frequencies and call sign of others you communicate with?"

Joe proceeds to do so. The President then comes back in.

"The range and use of our radio is limited because of damage it received. Will you relay a message to the Vice President for me."

"I would be honored to sir."

"Tell him most of us here are alright. Ask him to give me as close as he knows our current population count."

After Joe records the message, they sign off for the time being. Joe then radios the Vice-President in Hawaii.

"This is Col Smith go ahead Phoenix."

"I need to speak to the Vice-President I have a message for him."

"He is asleep. Can I take the message for him."

"Well wake him up. I have a message from the President for him."

"Yes sir. I will sent a messenger for him. Please maintain this frequency. Is the President okay?"

"He says he and others in his shelter are alright. How are things there?"

"Deteriorating, how about where you are? Is the radiation count declining there?"

Joe does not get a chance to answer any of the questions as the Vice President cuts in.

"I hear the President is alive."

"Yes Sir and he wants you to as close as possible estimate the United States' current population."

"Thank God, who am I talking with?"

"This is Phoenix in North Georgia."

"Is the radiation there low enough that a aircraft could safely land?"

"At this time, you would only last for a few days outside."

"Is their an airport near you with a runway long enough to support the landing of a large jet?"

"Just a minute, my father would know more about that."

"This is Will Ferguson. The Polk County and the Rome Airport have five-thousand foot runways. Most aircraft should be able to land on either of these provided they are not over loaded and the runways have not been damaged."

"Can you check them out?"

"Are you planning to come here?"

"It is a possibility. So far your radio seems to have the capability to reach those we can not and we need a command post on the mainland."

"We will check the Polk County Airport first as it is closer to us. Rome received a direct hit during the war and we must pass through there to get to its airport."

"Do you have protective clothing and chemical detectors?"

"Yes sir. We have protective clothing, radiation detectors and chlomatographs chemical detectors but I will not ask my people to spend much time outside until the radiation level is lower."

"I understand. Let us know as soon as you have the airport information."

"We shall. Over and out."

"We need two volunteers to recon the Polk County Airport and the ones who went out earlier can not go. Who do we have with aviation experience?"

"Henry and his daughter Leigh are the only ones I know."

"That's enough the reason I want two to go is in case one gets in trouble. Call for Henry to come up here."

John tells Will.

"I don't have any airport experience, but I volunteer to go with him."

"Good I don't want to send a man out with his daughter. If something happened to one of them, emotions could cause both not to make it."

Henry comes in and is made aware of the situation. He volunteers to go.

"We will wait until it rains again before going. Outside the radiation is still high and as you know if exposed for too long you will get sick. We really don't know how much protection the suits give. If you come across any obstacles on the way turn around and come back and we will try a different route the next day. Do not take any chances."

Will has asked Billy to have a special service that evening to thank God that the president and others are alive. Billy opens the service at 1700hrs that evening.

"As all of you know, the president and others with him are alive. I have called this service not only to thank God for that, but also to thank him for the many blessing he has bestowed upon us. Lets all sing the old hymn <u>Praise God Almighty</u>.

Led by Billy the congregation sing. Then Billy continues.

"Let's pray. -- Heavenly Father we come together to praise you and to thank you for all you have done for us. Without your protection, we know none of us would be alive tonight and we humbly thank you for this. We thank you that you have allowed the President and those with him to survive. We pray you give him and all of us the strength needed in the days to come. Amen."

"Billy if I may I would like to ask God another favor. God please we could really use some rain."

As if in answer to the prayer, suddenly John who is watching the outside monitors and has been listening to the meeting calls from the Control Room.

"Everyone I can't hardly believe it. It has just started to rain ."

The next morning Henry and John depart on the ATV's. Will has Henry's video transmissions shown on the large screen in the assembly area and most residents are watching. The Control Room is also watching John's video on another screen. There are wrecked cars all along the way and when they reach Cedartown the sight is awful there are wrecks with skeletons everywhere. Most of the buildings are destroyed. It appears mostly by fire.

Weaving their small vehicles through the carnage they reach the airport in about an hour. There they ride spread out down the runway.

"Will, do you see this I see no damage to the tarmac as of yet."

"What are your radiation readings? Henry, "Around 30."

"Is there room at the end to extend the runway?"

"Yes, it appears to be flat dirt for at least a couple of thousand feet to the east. To the west is another story it is just a major drop-off."

"Come on back now and don't stop for anything. You have been out there over a hour and a half already."

By the time they re-enter the shelter, their ATV's are near empty of fuel.. Will speaks to Fred.

"Fred get me the Vice President in Hawaii."

Before long the V. P. is on the radio and Will briefs him.

"The runway at Polk County Airport is in good shape and

the ground is level far beyond the pavement."

"This is good news. I have just come from a meeting where we agreed if the runway was useable we would attempt a flight there."

"We had a good rain last night but the ground is still radioactive."

"It will take a few weeks to assemble and deploy. Is there anything you need us to bring?"

"Some fresh fruit, vegetables and meat would be nice and our gas generators are out of fuel"

"I will see what I can do. Would you contact the President and let him know our plan."

"Yes, out for now. -- Fred see if you can contact the president and give him this news"

"Hello Phoenix were you able to contact the Vice President?" Fred, "Yes sir."

Fred then briefs the President on the Vice President's plan.

"Sounds good. keep me posted." Fred, "Yes sir, out."

The shelter is alive with excitement. The Vice President was maybe coming to their abode. The ladies immediately begin to form committees and make plans. That night Teresa and Will discuss this.

"Will we are all excited about the Vice-President coming. The girls are planning to greet him royally."

"I hope they don't overdo it. He still might not come."

"Well just in case, they want to be properly dressed. Is there anyway we might get dresses or cloth to make them."

"Give me a few days and we'll see what can be done."

The next week the only area testing positive for radiation is the ground and its within acceptable limits. So, Will agrees to let Kamilah, Bienca and Christine go toward Cedartown in search of materials. Bobby also goes with them. He is to see if any service station still has gas and figure out a way to retrieve it. They use two ATV's with trailers and are not to stay out over three hours. Bobby and Kamilah each wore helmets with video cameras so those in the assembly area could watch their progress. The girls get really excited when they discover the Wal-Mart building outside of Cedartown is mostly intact. The sight they find upon entering chills them to the bone. Partially decayed bodies are all over the store. They quickly filled their trailers with material, sewing machines, underclothes and dresses off the rack then asks Bobby to meet them out front of the building. Bobby has found plenty of gas and now he must bring an electrical generator with which to operate the pumps. Will and Gary meets them as they entered.

"Dad, although the buildings are gone there is plenty of gas but we have to use our generator to operate the pumps if they will still work."

"In case they don't, can you two rig up a pump to do the job?"

Gary is running over in his mind how this can be accomplished. He answers his dad.

"If we can find what we need. There was a hardware store on South Main. We should be able to find pumps and other things there."

"If the weather is good, tomorrow use our only reserve ATV and give it a go."

They then go to where the girls had parked and problems are stirring. Julia is raving at the girls.

"You three are nothing but thief's you have robbed Wal-Mart and should be punished for it. You took things that belong to others and did not pay. You shouldn't have."

The girls are defending their act and others are getting into the action. Will tries to calm everyone down.

"WAIT, EVERYONE LISTEN TO ME. -- There is no longer a Wal-Mart or for that matter any other businesses in existence. Money is no longer any good and even if it was there is no one to give it to. At this point we must salvage for our needs. This is not stealing as I said there is no one except ourselves to steal from. - Julia all of us wish this wasn't so but it is and we must accept it and go on. Now let that be the end of this discussion."

Julia begins to cry and walks away with her head down

"Mary Ann and Carmon will you two please go and console her? I understand her feelings and am sure you do also. Now the rest of you lets continue to work together as we have been and please work out kinks by discussion not by screaming. Shame on the ones who were so rough on Julia. Each of you should go and tell her you are sorry."

AIRPORT CONSTRUCTION BEGINS
CHAPTER EIGHT

By October, Bobby and Gary have salvaged enough gas to fill the generator tanks and store two-hundred gallons for the ATV's. Many trips to what had been Cave Spring and Cedartown has filled the food storage shelves with canned food. The ladies bring back personal things like lipstick, permanents for their hair and bathrooms items. Carlos finds a Humvee and is able to get it running. This allowed recon of a larger area. The distance a ATV could cover before running low on gas is limited. The humvee is also much safer than the much smaller ATV's.

The radiation is near a safe level and others decide to go outside and explore. Jerry goes out looks around and asks. "Is the large spring and its park in Cave Spring safe to visit. Joe, "I was down there yesterday and there are clear areas."

"Lets have a picnic in the park tomorrow."

"That sounds like a good idea but I suggest you wait until we can clear the bodies along the way. It would be upsetting to view them and then go have fun at a picnic. I have been planning to organize a group to bury them but there are so many. I have been putting it off. I will try to start tomorrow. I saw a backhoe the other day and wonder if we could get it going?"

Will has heard the conversation and interjects.

"Why don't You, Carlos, Gary and Bobby give it a try. Between the four of you, I would be surprised if you didn't."

The other shelters are briefed on the action of Shelter One.

They have also began to explore their areas and bury bodies. Everyone reports the same findings almost total devastation everywhere they go. Most are able to replenish their food supply and other much needed items. Bobby briefs them on how he and Gary had rigged up a pump to salvage gas. Unfortunately only five other shelters were still communicating with each other. Will could but wonder the status of the rest.

After the backhoe is repaired, the grim task of burying the massive number of dead begins. Mass graves are a necessity. No caskets are available so the bodies are wrapped in anything the burial detail could find. It resembles the pictures they had once seen of Black Plague victims. Billy holds ceremonies over the burials as best he can and many from the shelter attend. Even with the backhoe it takes weeks to complete this distasteful task.

Some decide to check Rome and try to get to the airport. They are unable to enter Rome by highway 27 from the South as the bridge over the Etowah River is severely damaged and debris covers its remains. The bridge at South Broad is the same way They climb Myrtle Hill and view what had been downtown Rome. It is just a pile of rubble. The bridge over the Coosa River at the Community of Coosa is damaged but passable, once a few wrecked cars are removed. They are unable to get within miles of Rome on highway 20 because of the destruction. Nothing is left of what had once been a thriving city. As there are many others things needing attention, it is decided to wait until later to try Rome's bypass.

Will decides to go around Rome to the Northwest and try to reach the airport. He and Henry attach a trailer loaded with a barrel of gas behind the humvee and started out. A trip that before would have taken an hour takes four. Everything along the way is destroyed and often they have to go off the road to get through. Arriving at the airport, they find the runway is filled with debris of all kinds and all structures in the area are, just gone. It would take a bulldozer to open the runway here. They return to the shelter feeling down.

Will decides it is time for Jerry's picnic. It is getting late in the year and soon it will be too cold for it. He informs the other shelters of their plans and invites everyone to join them. So on the first day of October they load their trailers with goodies and using all the vehicles head for the park. To everyone's surprise over four-hundred people show up.

The radio in one of the shelters had been damaged by the war and another had no radio. The one without a radio had sent a recon to the other and received the latest news. These shelters were located in Flagpole Mountain approximately five miles from Shelter One. They had thought they were the only survivors. The antenna and radio had been repaired in time to hear about the picnic and they had decided to surprise the other shelters.

Jubilation reigns as hugs, handshakes, smiles and crying for joy fill the park. It is a beautiful sunny day. They laugh, play games and frolicked all day long. A good time is had by all.

Speaking to the crowd, Will makes a proposal.

"God has allowed us to live. Notice the Church here although in need of repair it is still standing. I would like to see a joint effort to restore it. What do you say?"

A roar of approval goes up from the group.

"Billy is the preacher from our shelter do you approve of him leading the effort." Once again it is approved.

"Let him lead us in a prayer and then we have business to discuss."

"Heavenly father we humbly thank you for letting us and others live. We will now attempt to earn this reward. I ask that you strengthen us for the trials yet to come, amen."

Will then makes a request.

"Before we leave today would all of the shelter owners help form a committee for the good of all. This committee will meet near the church in an hour."

The appointees meet and each gives a report on the static of their shelter. Shelter Four's owner who was from Rome had sent his family but had stayed to protect his property from looters. Shelter Three's owner from Cedartown had done the same but showed up after the war started. He later died from radiation poisoning. Shelter Five, Shelter Seven or Shelter Eight owners nor their families had made it to the shelters.

The committee find that by working together most of their problem can be solved. Then someone comments,

"Many in our shelter desire to leave and re-establish themselves at their old homes."

Joe has made himself aware of conditions for many miles near Cave Spring. He tries to convince people to think of the potential consequences if they leave their shelters at this time.

"The radiation is still high enough in some areas that continual exposure may result in sickness or even death and no medical care will be available wherever they go."

Will then adds to Joe's warning.

"I understand the desire to go home. I am sure each wonders what they will find there. However, winter is coming soon and it will probably be another bad one. I suggest everyone wait until next spring. It will be much safer to leave then."

A lady comes running up.

"I have just heard the Vice President is coming here. Is this true?"

Standing on the steps of the church Will speaks to everyone.

"May I have everyone's attention please. The Vice-President and a contention from Hawaii may be coming to the Polk County Airport. We do not know exactly when but will let everyone know as soon as we do. Joe will brief your representatives on all we know about the world situation and they can brief you when you return to your shelters."

This really seemed to energize the crowd. The ladies who had not known of the potential visitors move among themselves already beginning to make plans.

Will then asks the committee for help.

"I have no idea how many planes will be coming. The Polk County is useable but the runway is of minimum length for them to land.-- I wonder if among us we have the capability of extending it?"

Ed from Shelter Five then remarks.

"Can we each check with the members of our shelter and see what we can do?"

"That's a good idea. Today is Friday lets meet there Monday with all the equipment and manpower we can muster?"

Everyone agrees and Joe begins to brief those who didn't know of the things that had happened since the war.

The Vice Presidents party was preparing for the trip to Georgia and Will waits each day for a message saying they were on the way. Finely.

"Phoenix this is Hawaii." Diana, "Go ahead Hawaii." "We have been delayed and it looks as though it will be December before we can deploy."

Will interrupts and makes a request.

"Can I speak to the Vice President. I have a favor to ask of him."

"Speaking what can I do for you."

"My nephew Doctor Robert Munoz is to the best of our knowledge in Australia. He is in the Navy and the last we heard was aboard the USS Missouri. His wife, daughter and parents are with us. Is there any way you can check on him?"

"I will see what I can do."

"We are now well over four-hundred strong. Survivors from eight shelters met today for a picnic in the park. We agreed to try and extend the runway and will start on this

Monday. By the way, we now have plenty of gas."

"That is good news we also have heard from others but no one on the mainland except you. -- A Picnic in the park, uh. Out."

On Monday, a contingent of forty from Shelter One and Two head for the Polk County Airport. As their near, they can see others already working, Jim from Shelter Four had owned a paving company prior to the war. He and several of his workers are in the same shelter. Since the picnic, they had searched out and found paving equipment and supplies that had belonged to the county and others. The extension of the runway is underway. Will greets with a smile.

"This is great Jim, just tell us where you need us."

"First I need to know what all you plan to do and how long do you want the runway?"

"If you could extend the runway to ten-thousand feet anything could then land on it. A taxiway on one side would help clear the runway for others to land. Lee is a Aeronautical Engineer and can advise you on thickness, width, and so forth. Leigh will you work closely with Jim?"

Leigh nods her head yes and Will continues.

"I think we also have people skilled it what it will take to construct at least one good building, if we can salvage the supplies to do so."

Will has the progress reported to the President and Vice-President daily. After two weeks things seem to be going well.

"Diana inform the Vice- President the runway will be ready by Mid December and a parking area shortly after."

"This is phoenix calling Hawaii." "Go ahead Phoenix."

Diana passed the news and is surprised to hear what comes next.

"This is the Vice President. The people of Hawaii have decided to form their own national government and have asked us to leave. We have until mid December. How many aircraft can you handle?

Will now takes command of the radio.

"Sir this is Will bring everyone you can. We will handle it somehow. Our people will work during all the daylight hours on the airport."

" What is left of our Navy has also been told to leave Australia and other ports where they had taken refuge. They have been allowed to refuel, given minimal supplies and are heading for the mainland. Will you pass this information to the President?"

"Yes sir, out."

Diana try's to radio the President. At first with no luck, then after several attempts

"This is the President brief me on the latest."

Diana does and the President responds.

"Ask the Vice-President if the Navy has provisions to

make it to Savannah. Tell him we need to regroup as near to each other as possible." Diana, "Yes sir, out."

Once again the Vice-President is contacted and responds.

"Tell the President I will get back to him on that."

Will goes over with Diana what must be done and suddenly begins to laugh.

"Well Diana our work is cut out for us. We must not only built a major airport over night but also a city to house those who are coming. When I was in the Air Force a sign on my desk read the impossible we do today miracles take a little longer. Well now we certainly need a miracle.

I have always heard the South would rise again but I never dreamed it would be this way. Open the intercom so everyone can hear then contact all the shelters and inform them of our quest. Tell them we need every able bodied man and woman they can muster to report to the airport in the morning. I am going to talk to Jerry and see about feeding them on site."

Will then goes to the kitchen to find Jerry.

"Jerry make a list of everything you need to setup a kitchen to feed over four hundred at the airport. It is an emergency."

"I will do my best."

"Either Bobby or Gary will pick up the list later tonight."

Will then goes to talk with Bobby, Gary, Joe and Henry.

"At 0600hrs, we must go and find materials to build a eatery for the airport and the equipment for it. Of the several restaurants that were in Cedartown, hopefully we can find what we need. -- Gary and Bobby take some men and work on this. Henry there once was a helicopter parked off highway 27 South of Summerville. Use the Humvee and take six men with you if you find one load it on the trailer and bring it back here. Leigh and the mechanics hopefully can make it operational. Henry I hope you still remember how to fly one. -- I will go to the airport and try to setup crews in shifts."

Carlos and others have been able to return several vehicles to working order and they will for sure come in handy now. The next morning everyone in the shelter loads up and heads for the airport.

Vehicle after vehicle arrive at the airport loaded with people. Will stands in the back of a truck with a bullhorn and calls everyone to assemble around him.

"As you know, we have been asked to do what some might think is impossible, but with God's help we will accomplish what must be done. Many lives are depending on you. I don't know how many are coming, but there will be a lot of um. We will need to work two shifts starting at daylight and going until dark. If any of you have paving experience please report to Jim so he can setup two crews. -- Jim take your people and go ahead. Completing the extension of the runway is now critical."

Jim sees the number of volunteers coming toward.

"Will, with this many men, I will run three shifts. I know where there are enough portable lights to allow us to work at night."

"Great, thanks Jim. -- Do we have anyone who has lead a crew in a major construction project?" Several hands go up. Will, "Come and stand to one side of me....... We need each of you to form a crew. Be sure to include a plumber and electrician if possible, but unless necessary to fill a crew don't select your shelters representatives."

Eight crews of twenty-five men each are formed and Will briefs the Crew leaders.

"We must work daily from dawn until dark so I suggest four crews work from 0700hrs until noon then everyone will have lunch and the other four crews work from 1300 until 18oohrs. This is about all the daylight we have. As soon as a kitchen is setup lunch will be served to everyone here at noon. You will eat breakfast and dinner at your own shelter. We now need to gather all the building materials we can find. Would each crew furnish men for this and let each crew try a different route."

Will had spent most of the previous night sketching basic plans for structures he felt were needed. -- After the search crews are selected they depart to look for materials.

"Now lets discuss our structural needs. I have a basic idea but no actual architectural drawings for you to work from. All I have are some sketches I drew. I think living quarters should be our top priority. I think hangers are out of the question. What do you think."

David wants a guess on numbers.

"How many are coming?"

"I don't know but from the sound of the Vice-President's

voice, there will be many. He asked how many we could handle. It could be hundreds.

David is ready to get going.

"Lets see your sketches."

The group discussed the drawings and Chuck comments.

"All of your buildings seem to be the same with the exception of one. What is it for?"

"I was getting tired when I drew that one. I laughingly sketched that building and you can see I labeled it the White House. To this Howard spoke up.

"I like it. My crew will build that one. I can find plans for it in what is left of the library."

It was Adam's turn to comment next.

"The rest resemble World War II open bay barracks. They will be faster to build that houses and we can built them from experience without plans. They will sleep about eighty per unit. I don't feel we will find the materials to make them two fancy."

Everyone agreed to this and it was decided to build barracks. Russell then reminds them of something Will had failed to mention.

"Each structure will need its own septic system. I am experienced in these and my crew will work on this."

Charles then does the math.

"That leaves six crews for the sleeping quarters. If we build three basic structures at a time, we can have the first three completed sometime in November, Weather permitting."

"Sounds good, get together, pick out a plot and go to it."

Douglas then asks the question Will was hoping not to hear.

"Suppose we are asked what we are going to pay the men for this work?"

"Their lives and the lives of their families were saved and no one paid anyone for this. This is their chance to perhaps save other American lives. That will be their pay. Money is no longer any good. We are faced with the task of rebuilding civilization in what was the United States. Only with each helping the other can we accomplish what must be done."

Joe has been listening silently as things unfolded. Now was time for his say.

"You will have those who don't want to work. When you do tell them to take their possessions and leave the area. We can not afford to have anyone plant the wrong thoughts in other minds. -- We are not trying to make anyone work. We are asking them to for the good of all. -- The remainder of our Air Force and the Vice-President is depending on us. Good luck, now lets roll."

Will then meets with the shelter representatives.

"Jerry is going to setup a kitchen out here. Bobby and Gary are gathering the equipment needed for this as we speak. He will feed three meals a day and needs a lot of help doing it.

Also we must construct a covered shed in which to prepare the food. Can each of you assist in furnishing people for this. He will need at least twenty cooks and servers and four men should be able to built a roof over their heads. -- The rest of us can help clean the debris from the area. Will someone take an ATV with a trailer and go in search of some trash cans."

At this time, Leigh drives up in a pickup.

"We are running out of paving material. Jim says unless he is re-supplied there will be no parking area. Also I wish we could add a couple of more inches to the existing runway. We don't know for sure it can stand the weight of a heavy aircraft."

Suddenly a noise not heard for a while, a helicopter is coming from the North. Everyone stops and goes to see who it is. The chopper lands on the runway and Henry steps out.

"We found two of these. The only thing this one needed was servicing and a new battery."

"You are just in time. Service the chopper and take Jim in search of paving material. By the way, where is the other one?"

"Its on the trailer and the guys are heading here with it now."

Everything was going so well that Will feared something would surely happen to break their string of good luck.

AIRPORT IS BUILT AT A HIGH PRICE
CHAPTER NINE

Jim and Henry locate the needed paving materials in Bartow and Gordon Counties and trucks are sent to retrieve it. On the first return trip, Earl the lead dump truck driver has an accident. He hits a car that had not as yet been removed from the highway. The loaded truck turns over spilling its load and blocking the highway. It happened at just the wrong spot and the other trucks could not pass. Henry sees it all from the helicopter and lands, picks up the injured driver and radios for help. Valuable time is lost as a backhoe must be driven the five miles to the accident to clear the road. Will hopes this would be the last problem they would face in completing the runway.

Dr. Reeves had setup a medical area at the work site. Until now he had only treated cuts and bruises but the man the helicopter brought in had a broken leg and possible internal injuries. He boards the helicopter and they head for Shelter One's Hospital. There Jennie x-rays Earl and finds besides the broken leg he has a broken rib and internal bleeding. Catherine and Jennie then prepare him for a needed operation. It took hours but the operation was a success. Earl would be okay but in the hospital for a few days.

The construction crews begins to return with materials they had found. It is immediately obvious they are far short of what is needed. Will suggests the kitchen shelter have first priority on the materials. Henry and David use the helicopter to once again go searching. David sees a steel beam outlet and they land to check.

"Wow, what luck there are enough thirty foot steel I-beams for the floor joist of all three barrack and then some. A large trailer or flatbed truck will be needed to transport them."

Henry radios this information back to the airport and they continue the search. What had been a Lowe's North of Cartersville was mostly intact. They land and find most of the materials needed are found there. This is much needed news.

They start back when disaster struck. As the helicopter takes off, a cable that Henry had failed to notice hooks a skid and the chopper crashes to the ground. Radioing the airport.

"We are in trouble here. We have crashed in the parking lot of the Lowe's in Cartersville and need help. David is out cold and I am not sure he is breathing. I am also hurt."

"Hang on help is on the way. Joe help Judy load stretchers and other medical supplies on the humvee and lets go."

Upon arriving at Lowe's they find Henry has pulled David clear of the chopper and then passed out. Judy gives them a fast check and tells Will.

"We need to get them to the hospital ASAP."

The injured are placed on stretchers and gently put in the back of the Humvee's. Judy works on David as they rush toward Shelter One. Will thinks to himself.

"We have got to find an ambulance and put it in service."

Dr. Reeves had started back to the airport. Joe sees him coming and stops him.

"Turn around we have two hurt bad."

While Jennie was x-raying David, Dr. Reeves checks Henry who had come to on the way to the hospital.

"What happened?"

"I crashed." He then looks at Will and asks, "The chopper?"

"It was destroyed but don't worry about it. We'll find another one."

Henry has a bad concussion, cuts and bruises but is going to be alright. Doctor Reeves tells him.

"After Jennie finishes with David she will x-ray your head and arm just to be on the safe side."

Jennie rolls David from x-ray into the Treatment Room.

"He has several broken bones. I posted the x-rays for you to look at."

Dr. Reeves goes in to read the x-rays as Will heads out.

"Well it has been some day. Come on Joe lets see what else might have happened at the airport."

Hank had taken charge of David's crew and had left for Lowe's. Will finds Carlos and inquires of him.

"On your roaming, have you seen anything that we can haul thirty foot steel I-beams on."

"How about the flat bed the paving crew used to haul the bulldozers. It is sitting down near the end of the runway."

"I had missed that. It will do just fine. Also, we need an ambulance, if you can find one."

Will decides to take inventory of the equipment they have salvaged. There was three bulldozers, four loaders with backhoes, six dump trucks, a large crane, a forklift, six pickup trucks, three two ton flatbed trucks, two Humvees, the cab with its flatbed trailer and eight smaller trailers. This was besides the paving equipment. -- The airport fuel tanks had been serviced but Will ponders.

"I wonder how long we can keep all of these going before running out of gas and diesel fuel."

Just then Bobby, Gary and their crews arrive. They only have one vehicle and its trailer Gary begins to report to Will.

"I thank we have found enough equipment to set up a kitchen that will feed an army."

Bobby interrupts.

"We had a problem. Kevin was trying to remove a large vent when it fell on him. His arm was cut bad. I wrapped it tight to slow the bleeding and Fred took him to the hospital."

"What a day of ups and downs this has been. -- Winter is almost here and the people will freeze in the barracks without some kind of heat. - Boys what do you suggest?"

Bobby makes a suggestion.

"We could move one of the shelter's largest generators here and install central heat and air, if we can find the units. There are plenty of small electrical heaters around in case we don't fine any heat pumps. I will work on it tomorrow."

Will problems keep running through my head.

"We need to construct a building for the work crews to get out of the weather. I will see if I can organize a crew for this. Meanwhile we need to roundup as many wood burning heaters as we can find and set them around the area."

Gary solves this problem.

"There are plenty of dead trees around to burn as fuel. I'll take care of this."

Just then the crew with the helicopter on the trailer drives up. So much had happened Will is leery of talking to them. John dismounts from the Humvee.

"Did Henry make it back with the helicopter?"

"Yes, but it later crashed Henry and David are in the Hospital."

"Are they going to be okay?"

"Yes, but they will be out of action for a while. How did your trip go?"

"Good, we had a flat on the trailer but were able to fix it. Incidentally we found a large number of eight inch concrete block and they are not damaged."

"Where are they and how many do you estimate are there?"

"About forty miles from here and there are several thousand."

"This is good news. When we go to pick them up will you lead the way?" -- John "Sure."

The afternoon construction crews were sorting through their building items as Will approaches them.

"Hey, John has found thousands of concrete block. Can you use them?" Charles, "You bet we can. We will put the walls up using block."

"Good, it is too late to go today so two of the crews can go and get them tomorrow.

Steve gives Will a report on their progress."

"We are laying off sites across the road to build the barracks. I have been meaning to check out the cement plant just down the road if we can get it working we could lay concrete foundations. I will come early tomorrow and see what I can do. It's too late now as it will be dark in an hour."

Each returns to their own shelter. It has been a day of progress, but at a price. At the hospital, the x-rays show Henry has a crack in the socket of his left elbow. This mean he would not be flying for a while even if a helicopter was available. He would be wearing his arm in a sling for at least three weeks. David would also be in the hospital for a while but was going to make it. Kevin had severed an artery and lost a lot of blood. Leonard had given him two pints, by transfusion. Will talks with Doctor Reeves.

"You have had a busy day."

"I thank everyone is going to be okay. If I can prevent

infection from setting in."

In the Control Room, Hawaii is calling.

"This is the Vice President. Admiral Smith has traded two destroyers for fuel and provisions for the rest of his fleet in Australia and they will be at sea in about a week. Our fleet here is leaving as we speak. The Hawaiian people have been most generous to us. As soon as you can accept us let me know and we will be on the way."

Will gives the Vice-Present a progress report.

"We have moved the UHF radio to the airport and have a retired controller to assist in your landings. We have no radar to help him but he says he can handle it. Most of the raw materials needed have been located and we have begun to build barracks. Can you give us the approximate number of aircraft and people that will be coming?"

"I will have Col. Carter gather that information for you. Can you still get through to the President?"

"Yes sir."

"Let him know about the Navy. Out."

Will speaks to Fred.

"Get me the president."

It takes awhile but finely the transmission is answered

"This is the President speaking go ahead Phoenix."

"Sir the Vice-President wishes you to know, the Navy in Australia and Hawaii are headed for the East coast as you directed."

"That is good news. Have him instruct them to check and see if the waterway is passable into Savannah's docks. If so have them dock there. If not have them anchor off shore in the area." --- "Yes sir. Out."

By the first of December, the runway and taxiway are completed, paving of the aircraft parking ramp is well underway, the barracks are built, a building as big as a hanger has been constructed and the White House is almost finished. Groups have been salvaging supplies from what had been the surrounding towns and the open building was converted into a warehouse. Some men had begun to build houses for their families in the area.

Just when it looked as though everything would be ready on time to greet the guest winter set in and slowed the progress. Since the war winters had been far more severe than before. The Northern hemisphere had cooled during the years of darkness caused by the radioactive dust. A blizzard hit the area and no one was able to leave their shelter for days.

This weather setback dampens the spirits of some of the workers and they want to wait until spring to finish the project. Will speaks to the other shelter representative by radio.

"We cannot force anyone to go outside but please stress how important it is that we finish what we started. Peoples are depending upon us. If we fail, they will surely die."

Ellen from shelter eight tells Will.

"Our people want to work but are snowed in and nothing we have will make it through the drifts."

"It has stopped snowing so in the morning my sons, nephews and I are going to try and make it to the airport in our Humvee. Once there, we plan to use the dozers to open the roads. We will keep you advised of our progress."

The trip to the airport proves the value of the Humvees. What had seemed like impassable areas the Humvees took in stride. Carlos, John and Fred had accompanied Bobby, Gary, Joe and Will. Fred and John had never operated a dozer or backhoe with a front-in-loader but they were about to learn. Gary, Joe and Bobby crank the dozers and start off while Will and Carlos gave John and Fred a fast lesson on the loaders. Soon they were following the dozers. The first day the roads to shelters one, two, three, four, five and six are opened. Shelter seven and eight are the furthermost distance away. Their roads are to be cleared tomorrow

It is cold, but enough workers show up to finish the job. By December 12, the airport and living quarters are ready. After notifying the Vice-President, Will decides to have a party and celebrate after all with God's help they have accomplished the needed miracle. Several men and women are musicians. They bring their instruments to the party and quickly form a band. Jerry and the Head Cooks from other shelters prepare a feast with canned meat and other items they had stored for just such an occasion. Will suggests everyone from all the shelters attend. The Vice President is informed the radio will be off and the party is on.

While people are eating and dancing unnoticed it starts to snow. The building has no windows and as it was cold outside no one had went out. Around midnight the first couple wishing to depart tries to open the door and finds they can't. The snow has piled up so high they are trapped inside. The dancing stops and people begin to mill about discussing the fix they are in. Some almost panicking. Tony the new band leader raps his makeshift baton on the wall to get everyone's attention,

"Apparently God wants us to celebrate a little longer..... Lets dance and be merry. How often have you had a chance to do so lately."

The band begins to play and once again everyone is alright. The party lasts until dawn and by then children and many adults have laid down anywhere they could and went to sleep. As soon as it is daylight outside several men began to try and open the door. Suddenly Diana is heard laughing out loud,

"Look the wind was from the North and this door on the South side is clear."

Everyone except the ones trying to open the North side door laughed. The sun is shining outside and it was going to be a beautiful day.

That evening the Vice president radioed,

"We are preparing to deploy and will be arriving on the morning of the eighteenth."

Joe asks for information.

"Did you get an estimate on how many were coming."

"It is impossible to tell, we have received word that the aircraft on Guam are also preparing to head your way. Can you handle it."

"We will do our best."

"We are in bad need of some medicines specifically insulin and pacerone are they available there?"

"I will check."

"The UHF radio is operational at the airport and a retired Air Force Tower Controller is prepared to bring you in."

"Good, I will pass this to Col. Carter. He tells me the aircraft will be landing approximately fifteen minutes apart."

"Tell him I would love to see the 1st TAC lead the way."

"I will tell him."

"We are looking forward to meeting with you face to face. Can you bring some fresh fruit, vegetables and a meal of meat for the over four-hundred here?"

"Are there any animals alive there."

"Only the breed stock of rabbits, chickens and fish we have in the shelters."

"I will do my best. Out."

Will tells Joe.

"Open our intercom and then radio the other shelters and ask if anyone has ever parked an aircraft. We need everyone that has or wants to learn how to meet us at the airport in the morning at 0900hrs. -- We are going to have company."

At the airport, Will is happy to learn over forty people who had been Air Force Aircraft Mechanics are among the people there.

"Have any of you ever worked Transit Alert?" Four hands go up.

"You four convert two pickup trucks into follow me trucks ASAP. Bobby will help you with the lights.

How many have worked on and parked aircraft?" Fifty-one step forward.

"Those with cargo aircraft experience stand over to the left please. -- Those who have been fighter aircraft mechanics step over to the right please. -- Okay, we are fully manned. Each group pick a leader and send him or her to me for a conference in the supply building. Those not yet assigned come with us."

At the meeting. other needs are filled.

"I am glad to see so many of you here. Do any of you have flight experience with aircraft?"

Frank and Allen step forward and state they are retired Air Force pilots. Frank is a Brigadier General and Allen is a Colonel.

"Good, now we need dozer operators."

Three hold up their hand and step forward.
"What I am about to say will sound odd but it is extremely important. We need the dozers parked between the runway and

taxiway. One half way down and the others one on each end. Now listen closely, we only have one runway and the planes will be very low on fuel. If anything goes wrong and one should block the runway no matter for what reason, it must be removed immediately many lives will depend upon on it. We don't have equipment to tow them so we will use the dozers to remove them from the runway. Frank, Allen or Henry will be on the dozer with you and will make the decision should it become necessary to push it clear. God knows I hope it doesn't. Frank, Allen do you agree with me on this?"

Frank and Allen both nod their heads yes and Frank tells everyone.

"With this many aircraft and under these conditions it's more a probability than a possibility that there will be trouble on the runway."

Hank enters and announces he is to represent the cargo aircraft mechanics, Melvin is to representing the fighter mechanics and Sid Transit Alert.

"Guys we are fixing to do what has never been done. It is a miracle from God that we got this far. As you know we will need chocks and ladders. Ladders for the fighters should not be a problem as there should be plenty to be found in the area. The pilots should have the safety pins with them please make sure they are installed. People who are unaware of the danger will be crawling all over them once they are all parked.

Hank, Melvin and Sid please go with Leigh she will advise you as to what spots are to be setup for what type aircraft. There is no turnaround space for the larger birds so have them come straight in. Hopefully we have enough space if not after the parking ramp is filled park them one behind the other on the taxiway. - Sid make sure your truck tires are clear of debris and don't drive off the tarmac until after all the aircraft are down."

Carlos, Bobby, Gary and Joe are waiting for their assignment.

"Carlos please have a pickup truck washed and checked for debris on the body and in the tires. Bobby and Gary we will need people to police the runway and taxiway and make sure they are clear. They will not be familiar with why they are doing it so tell them even a small rock ingested by a jet engine can do a lot of damage. - Joe I need you to handle security. Use some of your people and ask the other shelter representatives to furnish the rest. Rope off an area at least two hundred feet from the runway. People not directly involved in the recovery must be kept a safe distance away."

Jerry has been waiting patiently.

"How many am I going to have to feed?"

"I don't know get as much help from the other kitchens as you can and see if you can fix something for several hundred."

"It may be just beans, rice and cool-ade,"

"That will do just fine."

For the first time, Will is confident. He feels God is surely directing the whole operation. They are going to accomplish their mission. The airport is capable of handling a large number of all type aircraft and it is fully manned with skilled personnel.

HERE THEY COME AND THERE THEY GO
CHAPTER TEN

"Hawaii calling Phoenix."

"Go ahead Hawaii."

"This is Col. Carter. Is Will available?"

"This is Will go ahead Colonel."

"I hope you remember how to park me. I am coming in first."

"Don't worry, I have some of today's troops waiting for you. We have a five-thousand yard parking ramp just follow the Transit Truck there will be a mechanic waiting to park each of you."

"Sounds like your Air Force experience has stuck with you."

"Some things you never forget. Do you know how many birds and people are coming."

"I wish I knew. The aircraft stationed here and a civilian airliner are coming with us. We are bringing as many military families as we can safely put aboard the aircraft. The Vice-President is trying to convince the others and the civilians outside the base that the 141's will return for them. Thousands who were tourist here when the war stranded them are wanting to return home."

"I understand. Are you ready to copy co-ordinance?"

"Go ahead."

"Latitude 34 degrees 01.12' north, longitude 85 degrees 08.79' west at an altitude of 973 feet. The runway runs WNW to ESE and there is a beacon. Using UHF a retired Air Force Air Controller will bring you in.

"Thanks this will make it easier to find you. I'll see you in the morning at approximately 1000hrs your time. Over and out."

Everyone from all the shelters are at the airport by sunup. The mechanics and Transit Truck take their positions. Bobby and Gary's crews police the tarmac for debris, bulldozers are in place and the security force keeps the crowd back a safe distance. Will and Carlos wait with Kelly the controller.

"A slight wind is coming from the Northwest so I am going to direct them to approach and land from the South. God has blessed us again. Although it is cold. It is a beautiful sunny day."

Tensions begin to rise when at 1000hrs the aircraft have not been heard from. People began to mutter among themselves. Everyone is speculating as to what had happened to prevent the arrival of the aircraft. Everyone that is except those familiar with the many aspects of flight that could be in play. Weather or mechanical problems could have delayed their departure. They might not have been able to catch the jet stream just right or once over land they may have ran into a headwind.

Then Kelly hears.

"Phoenix this is the 1st TAC we will be in your area in approximately fifteen minutes. Landing instructions please.

"Roger I read you five by. The air is clear of clouds and the surface winds are approximate five to ten knots from the Northwest You are approaching from the West and I need to bring you in from the Southeast. Pass south of the runway and peel off to land from the southeast."

"Roger and I wish to pass over the runway before I land."

"I understand, bring um home."

Soon after four F-22s aligned one behind the other pass over the runway doing victory rolls one after another. The people are caught off guard as they didn't hear them coming. There is quiet a commotion in the crowd as they try to figure out what had just happened. Will smiles and says to Kelly and Carlos.

"They certainly have earned the right to do that. These pilots survived the war and now are coming home."

Will walks to the first parking ramp as transit leads in the first aircraft. He places the ladder against the aircraft and climbs up to greet the pilot.

"Col. Carter I presume."

"Will help me out of this thing I am not as young as I was three years ago."

Will laughs and lays the shoulder straps back over the seat.

"The pins."

Colonel Carter hands the safety pins to Will who gives them to the ground crew as he descends the ladder.

As they shake hands.

"I didn't expect to find a fully manned facility."

"We don't do things half way around here."

"There are mechanics and parts on a C-141 about an hour behind us. They will be happy to see how your men have helped them out."

"I thank they can skip the post flight today. There will be plenty of time for inspections later. By the way, the men who parked you are all volunteers. Everyone is happy to see someone else that survived the war."

The other F-22s lands as Colonel Carter and Will walk toward the supply Building.

"Lets go inside I bet you are hungry. - Laughing, Our chef has prepared a feast of beans and rice for you. The rest of your crew will be brought here as they arrive."

Even Will is surprised. Jerry and the others have prepared casseroles from canned meat they had found in an underground shelter. The occupants had not survived to eat it. They were not worried it was spoiled because it was ice cold where they found it. Also canned vegetables, rice, beans and canned fruit were on the serving line. Will introduces each cook as they go down the line. Jerry is at the end of the line.

"Colonel I would like you to meet the man who has kept

us from going hungry."

"This is great. We must talk sometime. I need you in the Air Force."

Will is sadden by this, maybe the Colonel had not as yet accepted that there was no longer a United States much less an Air Force.

As the Colonel and Will begin to eat three more pilots are escorted into the building. They spot the food and head for it.

"You have been calling me Colonel and I calling you Will. My name is Ernest Carter. What is your last name?"

"Before the war, it was Ferguson. When the war started we all agreed the only to survive was to work together as a family, so we decided to become the Phoenix Clan."

"Well its nice to finely meet you Will Ferguson Phoenix

"I would consider an honor if you would allow me to join the clan and call me Ernest."

The aircraft continued to arrive at six per hour until eighteen F-22s have landed. Then the Airborne Command Post lands with the Vice-President aboard followed by four C-141s, two KC-767 mid air refueling aircraft and two civilian passenger aircraft. Will and Ernest go to greet the Vice-President. Who had just got off the aircraft and was kissing the ground. Ernest smiles and tells Will.

"I felt like doing that myself."

The Vice-President extends his hand.

"You must be Will. I am amazed at what you have accomplished here."

"Not me sir, the others that you are going to meet constructed everything you will see here."

At this time Sid drives up, "Is that all of them"

"We don't know yet. Be ready and tell Hank and Melvin to keep their men in position for now. I will keep you informed as I know."

"Wait until you see the food laid out inside." Laughing "I thank they have been eating better than we have."

"Ernest will you take them inside I will be in as soon as I can."

Will see Carlos standing by with the pickup and motions for him to come over. They then go to those who have been watching and now want to cross the runway and greet the visitors. Joe and his men are having trouble restraining them. Will stands up in the back of the truck and hollows.

"Calm down their are others on the way and we are not sure exactly when they will get here. -- Carlos make sure the runway is clear then drive over and ask if the Controller has heard from them yet. I will stay here while you go."

Just as Carlos starts back a group of four F-22s pass over head.

"See why you must stay where you are for the time being. Believe me you will be allowed to cross as soon as it is safe to do so. I have got to go talk with these pilots and then maybe I will know more, so please wait here."

This seemed to appease the crowd somewhat.

After the four aircraft landed Will and Carlos cross the end of the runway and drive to where the aircraft were being parked. As soon as the first pilot alit Will approaches him.

"Welcome Colonel, I'm Will. Do you know how many more are coming."

As they shake hands the Colonel answers.

"I am Carl Yeager from Guam. We stopped in Hawaii to refuel and when we left six more F-22s and four C-141s were preparing to depart. The other F-22s are about fifteen minutes behind us and our refueler will be close behind them."

"The mechanics will show you and your men to the kitchen. The Vice-President and others are already there."

As they look for Hank and Melvin, Carlos and Will are shocked at the number of men women and children getting off the Cargo aircraft. Will informs Hank and Melvin,

"We do not have enough parking space. When the spaces become filled, setup on the taxiway and park one behind the other.-- Let Sid know the next time he comes in."

Hank and Melvin shake their head in disbelief.

Will and Carlos go back inside to talk to the Vice-President.

"Sir there appears to be hundreds of civilians off loading

from the cargo and passenger planes."

"We brought as many of the airman's families as we could with us and the civilians I had no control over."

"We have not build enough barracks to house all of them but let me talk to the Shelter Representatives and see how many they can put up. We will handle it somehow. I will get back to you."

Will, waited for another bird to land and then crossed the runway to talk to the Representatives each agreed to take in twenty-five women and small children, plus ten girls and twenty boys over the age of ten. Most would have to live in the dormitories.

Will reports this to the V.P.

"We can put up four hundred or so women and children. They will have to stay in dormitories but will be warn, fed and have medical attention available to them. The men will have to stay in the barracks until better arrangements can be made."

"I feel they will be thankful for your hospitality."

"For now, we need to bring them in here and feed them as long as the food last."

Ernest has something to show Will.

"I know by now it will take a lot to surprise you but I hope you are happily surprised at what one of the 141s is loaded with. Come and let me show you."

As they enter the 141, Will is overcome by what he sees.

The first is a live bull and two cows. Then crates marked meat and others marked vegetables or fruit. The aircraft is filled from front to rear with food supplies.

"We can sure use some of this."

" Its all yours. We have a supply for ourselves on another aircraft."

Will immediately gathers the shelter representatives and asked them to have the items evenly divided and taken to the eight shelters. Ellen eyes the cattle. It has been a long time since anyone has had a steak dinner.

"What will we do with the cattle?" Will, "Leave them here for tonight. We will figure that out tomorrow."

Suddenly a loud noise comes from the runway. A F-22 has blow a tire while landing and its right strut collapses. It spins onto the edge of the runway blocking the aircraft scheduled to land behind it. Hank and others run to check the pilot and remove debris from the runway. Frank orders his driver to clear the runway and everyone watches in awe as the F-22 is for all practical purposes destroyed as the dozer removes it from the path of the aircraft which are required to circle until the runway is cleared.

The runway is made safe and the other aircraft begin to land critically low on fuel. The last F-22 flames out as it touches down and rolls to the end of the runway. Hank's crew respond and push the aircraft from the runway onto the taxiway just before the cargo birds begin landing.

As soon as all the aircraft are down, Will asks Joe to let everyone come over. Hugs and handshakes go on for a good while. Will is glad the crews had built so large a utility building. It was coming in handy as over nine-hundred people are now crowded inside and everyone is able to eat something.

Everyone is tired from the days activity so sleeping arrangements are made and trucks loaded with women and children leave for the shelters. Each shelter sends someone to assign quarters. Their are mechanics, doctors, cooks and other trades represented with the new arrivals.

A man approaches Will.

"I am Doctor Smith. I have brought medical supplies. Where do you want them."

Doctor Reeves has just returned from the crash site.

"Hey, Leonard this man has something for you."

Leonard comes, greets Dr. Smith and they leave to get the medicine from the aircraft. Gary and Carlos lead the men to the barracks. Where one jokes.

"Just like home."

Each had brought a fold up cot with them and were happy to see they didn't need them as bunk beds were there for their use. Some go to the showers and others just go to bed. It had been a long and tiring flight.

The Vice-President looks at Will.

"I need to use your radio and report to the President."

"My sons will take you and Ernest to our shelter in the

humvee. Sleeping arrangements have been made for you there." Laughing, "Don't expect them to be plush how."

"What about my staff and security people?"

"They will have to sleep in the barracks. There is no need for security here and there is no more room in the shelters."

Will could see the Vice President was unhappy about this but that was the way it must be.

"Carlos and I will be along shortly."

Will goes outside and talks to the controller.

"Have you heard from anyone else?"

"No I guess that's all of them."

"Jump in the truck and we will go tell the others they can wrap it up and get something to eat."

Hank and Melvin decide to spend the night at the airport in case others arrive later that day or in the morning. The Airport's Maintenance Crews then return to their individual shelter. It has been quiet a day. As they drive home, Will reflects with Carlos on the days happenings.

"Today a hand full of people accomplished a miracle. Thank God for his help. The weather sure was nice."

Leonard has meantime taken Dr. Jones to the hospital.

"I am amazed at everything I have seen today. I surely did not expect to find a staffed and operational hospital. They call you Leonard are you a doctor?"

"Everyone here is called by their first name. I am a General Practitioner but here I have been the Surgeon and what ever else was needed. Let me show you to your room it is the only one not in use and the bathroom is down the walkway. Tomorrow after you have rested, I would appreciate it if you would look in on the patients. We have had several accident injuries."

In the Control Room, the Vice-President asks Joe.

"Will you see if you can get the president."

"This is Phoenix calling the President's Shelter."

"This is the president. I have been waiting to hear from you."

"Frank this is Jerry. We have arrived in Georgia."

"How many are with you?"

"Several hundred and a fleet of aircraft."

"Were all of you able to land safely."

"Yes, you would not believe the facilities and trained personnel here."

"That's great as soon as the Navy is positioned off Savannah they need to recon the International airport there. That is a large port city and more than likely ample supplies can be found to get us through the winter. If the airport is useable, I want all of us to assemble their and get the United States reorganized. With me are experts from every governmental department. You know my location. Have a Navy helicopter pick me up as soon as it is practical."

"Yes sir. Out."

Joe laughs to himself at the presidents comments.

"Politicians never cease being politicians. I wonder now many people are alive to be governed?"

"Colonel can we make it to Savannah."

"Not without fuel and I am sure some of the birds have serious maintenance problems. The least of which being bald tires. Tomorrow I will debrief the pilots and the maintenance crews will inspect the aircraft. I will know more then."

"Joe can you get through to the Navy?"

"I will try they have not answered for the last week. - Any U.S. Navy ship, this is phoenix come in please."

After several attempts, he receives a response,

"This is the Missouri how can I help you."

"This is the Vice-President is Admiral Smith aboard your ship?"

"Yes Sir. Stay on this frequency and I will patch you through to him."

"Phoenix this is Admiral Smith."

The Vice-President greets him and then passes the

presidents message. To which, the Admiral remarks.

"I will do what I can. We have had a little trouble on the way. A Chinese sub apparently did not know the war was over. He caught us by surprise, sunk a destroyer and crippled a carrier before we sank him. I will notify you when we are off Savanna. Out."

Once again Joe wonders at the Admiral's words and speaks to all who hears him.

"Will men continue to kill each other until their is no one left to kill?"

Overnight the weather turns bad and the area receives over a foot of snow. Everyone is trapped where they are until the dozers can open the roads. Hank has never driven a bulldozer so he recruits one of the new arrivals. He accompanies the new driver and directs him to Shelter One. As soon as the road is opened, Earnest and Will use a humvee and leave for the airport.

At the airport they find, CMSgt. Sullivan from the 1st TAC and CMSgt. Edwards from Guam two Maintenance Superintendents had worked together and setup an office in the supply building. The pilots had been debriefed and their men had completed a preliminary check of the aircraft. It had not been possible to perform a proper inspection because of the weather.

Sullivan briefs Colonel Carter.

"Six F-22s are grounded and can't be made flyable without parts and several others have badly worn tires. Since we don't have the parts to repair the two engine problems we are cannibalizing from these birds and are putting others back in commission. The cargo birds have minor problems but are flyable."

Col. Carter is pleased with this report and returns to the shelter to brief the V.P. Who asks.

"Will is their a source of jet fuel available?"

"No but there are a couple of airports within one-hundred miles that might have had some survive. When the weather allows we will check."

"We need to depart as soon as possible. Among other reasons we are depleting your store of supplies."

Will then questions Ernest.

"Does either of the tankers or cargo birds have sufficient fuel to safety make it to Savannah?"

"I don't know what do you have in mind?"

"If one could and there was a fuel supply there, it could service and then bring a fuel truck back here."

"Will go with me to talk to Sgt. Edwards."

At the airport, Ernest talks to CMSgt Edwards.

"Sgt. Edwards is their enough fuel in one of your birds to safely make it to Savannah?"

"It would be close I wouldn't want to see a crew chance it."

Will then comes up with a plan.

"What if you drained the remaining fuel from the other birds and put it into one?"

"That might work. I will need some equipment."

"My sons rigged the pump and tank they used to salvage the gas we are now using. I will have them bring it and help you in using it."

" Sounds good, when can we start."

"I'll radio them and they should be here in about an hour."

That evening a radio message is received from the Navy.

"Phoenix this is Admiral Smith is the Vice-President available?"

"This is he. Go ahead Admiral."

"We successfully landed a helicopter at Savannah's Airport. The runways are clear and not damaged. There was no sign of life but there is a good supply of fuel and plenty of civilian aircraft there."

"Good, as soon as the weather allows a 141 will be headed that way."

"Will you be aboard this aircraft?"

"Yes I think I will."

"I will have a helicopter meet the aircraft and bring you aboard ship, out"

The morning of the twentieth of December, The sun comes out and the snow begins to melt. The loaders are used to clear the runway and the refueled C-141 taxis out for its flight to Savannah. It is carrying the Vice President, his staff and as many civilians as there is room for. Most of the shelter personnel are there to see it go. As it disappears in the distance Will thinks.

"And he didn't even say goodbye. I guess he was happy to get away from here."

The pilot had promised Colonel Carter.

"We will be back today if everything goes right."

Phoenix crews would not be needed to recover the aircraft when it returned but the Controller would be.

"Kelly can you be available this afternoon to guide him in."

"I will be here."

Sgt Edwards asks for a little more help.

"Will if your Transit Truck will lead him back in I would appreciate it. My Airmen will handle it from there."

"No problem."

Approximately six hours later the C-141 returns with a fully loaded fuel truck. The tankers receive enough fuel to make the flight and immediately depart for Savannah. Another 141 receives the rest of the fuel. The empty fuel truck is loaded back on the 141 and it departs again. Along with the second 141.

The next morning at 0800 hours the 141s can be heard in a distance, they land with a fuel truck each. The first person to leave an aircraft heads running toward the crowd of people.

Jennifer cannot believe her eyes.

"Look its Robert."

The entire Munoz family run to meet him. Robert grabs his wife and holds her tight as they kiss. He then hugs his daughter and greets the rest of the family. It is a happy day for the Munoz family.

The main tanks of the flyable F-22s are serviced this is sufficient fuel to take them to Savannah. The rest of the fuel goes into the remaining 141s and 767s. There is not enough for the Airborne Command Aircraft nor the civilian airline jets. They will have to be retrieved later.

All of the shelter residents are at the airport to say goodbye and wish the travelers a safe trip. All but one of the cargo birds taxi out and depart. This one stays to transport the mechanics who were launching the fighters.

Colonel Carter says his farewells.

"Will thanks for all you and your people have done for us. I will stay in touch and God willing you will see me again."

They shake hands, Ernest boards his bird and leads his

command down the taxiway. Each pilot salutes as they pass the crowd of people watching them go. Before long they are but a noise in the distance and then silence. The only sign they were ever there was the abandoned aircraft on the tarmac.

Will to anyone who happens to hear.

"May God continue to protect them. They are good people."

The shelter residents gather in the supply building to mull over what has just happened.

Bobby comments.

"It's almost like a dream we have all had. They were here and so soon they are gone."

CHRISTMAS AND UNEXPECTED VISITORS
CHAPTER ELEVEN

Will has called a meeting of all available personnel from all the shelters.

"Our visitors are gone and we must plan our own future. The cattle will be very important to us if we can keep them alive. Does anyone have any suggestions?"

Julian stands up.

"My family and I are farmers let us take care of them."

"Okay but what are you going to feed them. The grass is all dead and might not grow back for years."

"I have noticed several barns in the area. I will take them to the nearest one. Maybe some of the hay is still good."

"Where will you and your family live it is too far to travel back and forth from the shelter?"

"I don't know."

Howard responds to this.

"The white house is finished. I plan to move my family there in the spring but your family can stay there until then and there is a barn near it."

Bobby also tries to help come up with a solution.

"There are several places nearby that sold cattle feed. I bet we could find enough to at least feed them through the winter."

Gary remembers a possible source.

"There was a feed mill Southwest of Cedartown."

"Can you two help Julian find and store as much feed as the weather allows."

"We had better do it now because it looks like it could snow again any minute."

"Julian go ahead and take the cattle to the barn and the boys will start gathering feed. You will also need to keep a loader near by as you might need it this winter."

Kelly then declares.

"I doubt if we will have any visitors for a while but just in case my wife and I will stay here at the airport. We will portion off part of the downstairs area of one of the barracks for living quarters. This building is well stocked with supplies and a kitchen. If anyone needs something I will use the snow removal truck Carlos just brought in and make deliveries."

Hank then says.

"I thank my family will do the same."

"I suggest you use only the electricity necessary to insure you have enough gas in the generator to last the winter. I believe most of us are going to stay in the area after the winter. I would like to see us establish a town here. We already have a nice airport. If we live close enough together, each family could establish their own trade and we could barter for each others goods."

Martha gives her opinion on this.

"There are plenty of supplies available without that."

Adam has been quiet during previous discussions, but he responds to Martha.

"True there are ample supplies now but they will run out and then what will you do? Where will you get even a toothbrush? I thank Will's suggestion is a good one. He hasn't steered us wrong yet."

"Thank you Adam. -- We have the rest of the winter to think it over. Lets plan on a grand get together here next Easter. Everyone will know what they want to do by then...... Good luck this winter and if anybody needs help be sure to say so. In case I don't see you before the 25th have a Merry Christmas."

Gary and Bobby do not return to the shelter until after dark. They go directly to the Control Room.

"Dad it is really coming down out there."

"I know I was ready to organize a search party for you."

"Well I think we took enough cattle feed to Julian to last through the winter."

"I'm afraid this is going to be the worst winter we have experienced yet."

By morning, snow drifts cover the outside cameras. Joe

had closed the covers to protect the lens. Winter had truly come to stay for a while.

Will goes to the hospital finds and Robert, Leonard and Doctor Smith there.

Doctor Smith explains his presences there.

"My name is Gilbert. I decided to stay and hope that's okay with you."

"Okay, why I feel like hugging you. There have been times when Leonard has needed another doctor's help and now there are three of you."

Leonard can't restrain himself from commenting on that.

"Amen to that, Robert is an Orthopedic Surgeon and Gilbert is a Cardiovascular Surgeon and we have patients in need of both of their specialties . Among other problems, we have several heart patients."

Will smiles at Leonard.

"Yes, Teresa and I are two of them. - How are your injured patients."

"We have discharged all of them but David. I want to keep him under observation for a while longer."

In their roaming, Someone had found a large artificial Christmas tree and plenty of lights and other fixtures. The children are allowed to decorate it and they have a good time doing so. Billy forms a choir which sings as the children decorate. The shelter is filled with song and laughter. It is really beginning to look like Christmas.

The children come into the lobby on Christmas morning their eyes light up. They are in awe, they surround the tree and just stare at it. Presents are piled high around the tree. Before the weather had gotten too bad for it, their parents had roamed around until they found gifts for their little ones.

A big eyed young girl suddenly screams out.

"Look Santa Clause has found us."

Carmon and Mary Ann pass out the gifts and the children are allowed to open and play with their presents before breakfast.

Jerry once again had a surprise for everyone. He had stored away fresh eggs which the visitors had brought and was serving them this morning. Merry Christmas is heard through out the shelter. After breakfast everyone gathers in the assembly area and they sing Christmas carols. Then watch, Its A Wonderful Life on the big screen. - Later when the residents come down for dinner Tony and the band are playing Christmas Music. After dinner a Christmas party is enjoyed by all.

The weather becomes even worst. The cold northwest wind seems never to stop and snow piles so high it covers the entrance to the shelter. The temperature outside drops to fifteen below. Will was concerned about those at the airport. The Control Room had not been able to get through to them for over a week but there was no way to go outside and check on them. Finely around the first of March the weather begins to moderate. And the snow begins to slowly melt. A couple of days later John opens the outside camera lens and was thrilled by what he saw. He announces over the intercom, "Hey everyone look at this."

On the big screen they see a front end loader slowly removing the ice and snow from the shelter entrance.

"Its Hank and Kelly is sitting in a snow removal truck watching him."

Will and others rush to greet them. As soon as it is practical John opens the outside door. Hank and Kelly rush in.

"We have been worried about you. We thought the weather might have taken you."

"We thought the same about you. Our radio went out and we couldn't contact anyone. Have you been in contact with the other shelters."

"Yes they are all snowed in but okay. How about your wives, Julian and his family?" One of Julian's boys is sick. He has a fever. This is one reason we came he needs a doctor and the other kids are not too perky either."

"Can a humvee get through?"

"Yes, if you can get it started, after we dig it out from the mountain of snow covering it."

"You two go on inside and warm up.

Turning to the others Will says.

"I need two volunteers to uncover a Humvee and see if you can get it started."

Joe and Gary had brought heavy coats, caps and gloves with them to the entrance. They knew in advance it would be them to go out.

"Bobby go to Leonard and advise him we need help and tell him to dress warmly."

Within fifteen minutes The Humvee was running and ready. Gary and Joe come back in and Will comments

"It's hard to believe that thing started right up as cold as it has been."

Gary laughs and explains.

"I'm glad Bobby put the electrical outlet outside the door. I had placed an electric blanket over the engine to keep it from freezing, disconnected the battery and covered it also."

Will gives his son a hug.

"Good thanking, thanks son."

Just then Leonard comes running up,

"What's wrong."

"Julian's family needs you. I don't know exactly what's wrong but one has a high fever." The Humvee is running and one of the boys will drive you."

Joe tells Leonard.

"I'll do it lets go Doc."

At this time Hank and Kelly come to the entrance.

"We have to go now and get the vehicles plugged in before they freezes up."

"Have you warmed up any."

"Yes we had a coffee and Jerry gave us a thermos each to take with us."

"Take a video/radio helmet with you that way we can, not only talk to you, but also see the area as you talk. The helmets are hanging on the wall behind you."

Bobby hands them each a helmet.

"Go with God to protect you."

Later Joe radio's the shelter.

"Have gurneys ready we are coming with three sick kids."

They arrive soon after and Joe pulls the passenger side of the Humvee as close to the shelter door as possible. Catherine, Judy and Jennie have been waiting with gurneys. The children are rushed to the hospital where Gilbert is waiting. He and Leonard begin running test to determine what is wrong with the boys.

Will asks Joe about the others at the airport.

"The rest seem okay and dad you are not going to believe this. Not only have the cattle survived but the two cows were pregnant when they arrived here and Julian says they will calf in the spring. He said one of the cows was a beef cow and the other is a milk cow. He figures that in a few years there will be fresh milk and beef."

Will doesn't want to dampen the good news, but.

"That is if he can find food for them. Remember nothing is growing outside but the snow drifts."

After a few days Julian's kids are alright and running all around the lobby.

Gary watches them at play with the other kids.

"I think they got sick from being shut up in the house for so long."

Leonard, "That was part of it."

Will sends word to Julian and Jill their kids are alright and asks to keep them at the shelter until it warms up outside.

All winter Colonel Carter had contacted the shelter on a regular schedule to check on their status and brief them as to what was happening in Savannah.

In mid March he radio's in.

"Phoenix this is Col. Carter can you handle some visitors?"

"Our runway is currently under a blanket of snow. What type and how many aircraft are coming?"

"There will be five 141s, a refueler and three commercial jets. The Vice-President wants to make good on his promise to return for those stranded in Hawaii."

"Check with me tomorrow morning and I'll let you know how soon we can have the airport ready."

"Someone else wants to meet the people there. I will bring him when we come."

"Who is it."

"I can't promise anything yet. So lets wait and see. Out."

"John see if you can raise Hank, Melvin, Sid and Kelly on the radio."

This is accomplished and Will gives them the news.

"We have just been requested to accommodate turnarounds of some aircraft headed for Hawaii. What do I tell them?

Hank wants to know.

"When?"

"ASAP, Melvin, Hank what is the condition of the runway and taxiway?"

"We can have them cleared in a couple of hours, if it doesn't snow again tonight."

Melvin is ready for some excitement.

"I say bring them on. I am sure several of the men will be happy to get outside for a while."

"Sid are the transit alert trucks in commission?"
"Yes, me and the guys are ready for some action."

"Then I will tell them to come tomorrow afternoon, weather permitting."

That evening Will radios Ernest.

"If the weather is clear tomorrow, the runway will be ready by noon. Do you know this time how many people ware coming?"

"Sixteen aircrews and a few others."

"We can handle that. - I am sure you remember we don't have any fuel or deicing equipment here."

"That is taken care of. See you tomorrow about noon."

The next day is very cold but clear. Hank and Melvin start working on the runway at daybreak and by 1100hrs everything is ready to once again welcome visitors.

Kelly is in position and hears.

"Phoenix this is Ernest. We are twenty minutes out."

"Roger, the winds are at ten with gusts to fifteen from the Northwest the chill factor is well below zero. Approach and land straight in from the South. We will park you on the taxiway one behind the other as the parking ramp is covered with ice and snow."

"Roger, we are heading in."

The planes land with a five minute interval between them. Bobby, Gary, Carlos and Will are each driving a Humvee to transport the visitors to the supply building. Jerry and others have prepared lunch for approximately fifty. As the first 141 is parked and shuts down one couple disembarks first. Will steps out to meet them thinking it is Ernest but gets a surprise. It is President Dollar and his First Lady Laura who extend their hands.

"Are you Will?"

"Yes sir that's me." President, "I have been looking forward to meeting you and the others here."

Ernest and others leave the 141 and come over.

"Lets go inside before we freeze. We can greet each other there."

At the supply building everyone go in except Bobby, Gary and Carlos who go back for the flight crews. The airport personnel have their own transportation. Inside the President and First Lady shake everyone's hand.

"I am proud to be among you people. You have done America a great service."

"I know everyone is still cold so lets all have a warm meal and we can talk as we eat."

The First Lady leads them through the buffet and then they sit at a near table.

"Ernest brief me as to your plans."

"The ground crews we brought with us are at this moment off loading five fuel trucks and a deicer. We are going to depart for Hawaii as soon as the birds are refueled and made ready."

"I hope you plan on letting your men come in here, eat and warm up before you leave."

Ernest laughing.

"Okay Sgt. if you insist."

The President surprises everyone.

"Laura and I would like to stay here while the others make the trip, if it is okay."

"That would be nice as those in all eight shelters would like to meet you two. We have the perfect place for you to stay.-- Julian could the President stay with you in the White House?"

"The wife and I would be honored."

"The White House?"

"Yes, Howard's crew have built a smaller version of what was your residence in Washington."

The President shakes his head.

"I can not believe it. What other wonders have been accomplished here?"

"God blessed those of us here and allowed us to

accomplish a few small miracles."

President Dollar, "I truly believe it."

Ernest asks.

"Can you still contact anyone in Hawaii?"

"We converse with those who now live in what was the American Embassy on a regular basic. It seems many still hope to return to the mainland and others have decided to become Hawaiian citizens."

"Will you contact them and let them know we are on the way to fulfill the Vice Presidents promise to return for them."

"I'll be glad to but boy if it were me I would ask you to wait until spring."

The President answers to this.

"We need as many people as we can get on the mainland. As you know the population of the United States is critically low at this point. So, I decided to bring home as many Americans as we can as soon as possible. We also are searching by radio for others."

"There are still thousands in South and Central America."

"We are working on that. We have made flights to Mexico and Brazil but few Americans are there. We were however able to trade items from Savannah for fresh fruit and vegetables and have brought you two pallets of these"

"Great we can sure use them. Jerry get someone to drive the forklift and have them brought in here before they freeze."

"I'm on it."

The airport and aircraft crews enter and report the aircraft are ready to launch.

Earnest looks at Will and smiles then tells the crews.

"Have something to eat, warm up and we will be on our way. -- Will the crews will need a couple of days rest when we get there. We will radio our approximate return arrival time back here."

"You all deserve a day to frolic on the beach."

Less than an hour later the planes taxi to the end of the runway and takeoff. Of those who came only the President and First Lady remain at the airport.

Will inquires of Julian.

"How is your food supply?"

"We could use a few things. Especially enough of the fresh vegetables for a meal or two."

"Get with Jerry and he will fix you up with that and it would be nice if you invite the others who live here at the airport to dine with the president and your family tonight."

"Can do."

"Mr. President I am going to now take you and the First Lady to the White House for tonight. Weather permitting I will pick you up around 0900 tomorrow and take you to our shelter. The next day we will tour the other shelters. If that is agreeable with you."

"That's fine. - I noticed you called Colonel Carter by his first name and everyone here is addressed by their first name."

"Yes sir, when we first entered the shelters we agreed to become one family. We now are the Phoenix Clan. Our dream is to raise this area from its destruction much as the mythical Phoenix arose from the fire."

"And it is obvious you are accomplishing this. I would be honored if Laura and I could be a temporary members of your clan."

"It will be our pleasure."

"Great from now on call us Laura and Frank."

Frank and Laura are taken to the White House and as they approach Laura chokes up.

"Frank look it looks like the White House in Washington. I could just cry."

As they walk up to the door, Jill opens it.

"Come in before you catch your death of cold."

Once inside, Will does the introductions.

"Frank, Laura may I present Jill your hostess for the night."

Jill is stunned to see who her guest are. She stammers.

"It's, it's an honor to have you. My house is your house."

Will rescues Jill from her almost trance.

"Jill, Julian is bringing fresh vegetables and the others who reside at the airport for dinner tonight. Can you handle it or do you need some help?"

"Goo, good, we'll have a Dinner Party.

The President smiles at Jill and tells Will.

"Laura, Jill and I can handle it."

"Okay have a good night and I will see you in the morning."

"Are you not going to stay here tonight. We need to discuss this areas future."

"I have other duties. We can talk tomorrow. In this Clan, we are as one so if you will discuss your plans at dinner tonight. Anyone of us can speak for the other. We are a true democracy here."

At the shelter, Will instructs Diana.

"See if you can raise anyone in Hawaii."

After several attempts.

"Go ahead Phoenix, this is Hawaii."

"Am I speaking to a Government Official."

"I am Lee a Representative in our government. How may I help you?"

"There are several aircraft heading your way. Would you please announce over your news media that those wishing to return to the mainland should report to the airport three days from now."

This is good news to the Representative.

"I will be glad to. We are overcrowded and our economy is in a bad state. The more that leave the better."

"Thank you sir, out."

The next day Will uses a humvee and brings Frank and Laura to Shelter One. All residents not on duty have formed a reception line. Will introduces everyone by name as Frank and Laura proceed from one person to another. Afterwards the ladies and Laura meet in the assembly area and discuss woman issues and Will gives Frank a tour of the shelter. The first stop is the hospital where Frank meets Leonard, Robert, Gilbert and their staff. Leonard then guides him through their facility. Frank and Will then tour the complete shelter ending up in the Control Room where Frank talks with everyone on duty.

"I am amazed at what I have seen. Who designed and built this shelter for you?"

Joe is on duty and answers.

"Dad designed and oversaw the construction of the shelter's."

Frank turns to Will.

"I though you were a retired Maintenance Super."

Will smiles.

"I am one of them also."

"Are the other shelters the same as this one?"

"All except Shelter Two we'll go through the tunnel to that one later today. - We sold shelter blueprints and survival manuals to over one-hundred and fifty individuals and groups all over the nation. Most shelters were constructed prior to the war but many owners made unsafe changes to the plans or failed to stock properly. Some did not even install radios for communicating with others. They did this to save their precious money. Shortcuts to save the now worthless money cost most of them their lives. I still pray each night that some are still alive but unable to communicate with us."

"Why is it you are able to contact so many by short wave radio when others can not?"

"The difference is in our antenna. It is retractable and was underground during the war. When extended it stands over two-hundred feet above the hill we are inside."

"If I had just known, the government could have built this type shelter throughout the United States."

"I personally mailed a set of blueprints to you. I guess someone decided not to bother you with them."

Frank lowers and shakes his head.

Just then, a voice over the radio.
"Phoenix this is Ernest. Do you read me?"

John answers.

"Five by, what is your location?"

"We are safely in Hawaii. I thought I would check in before I hit the beach. -- Wish you were here."

"Ernest this is the President what is the status of your mission?"

"The Hawaiian Government is using the news media to alert everyone who wishes to return with us to report to the airport by 1000hrs tomorrow."

"Good. enjoy your swim and then inform us of your planned date and estimated arrival time here."

"Yes sir, out."

Frank now turns to Will.

"When it's convenient, I would like to gather the shelter residents and speak to them."

"Now is a good time as it's an hour before dinner. - Joe announce the President wishes to speak to everyone in the Assembly Area."

The President speaks to the assembled residents.

"First let me say, each of you are to be commended for

what you have accomplished here. You have taken the first steps in the restoration of our beloved country. You chose to call yourself the Phoenix Clan and have began to arise from the ashes of war, much as the mythical bird, the Phoenix. - Our entire nation must now rise from these same ashes. We are forming a new national government and I want you to be a part of it. I would like many of you to resettle. To those that relocate the Government will give each family the deeds to five-hundred acres, of any part of the United States not at this time claimed or occupied. - We must repopulate our nation."

A roar of approval goes up from the crowd.

"I would like all of you to return to savannah with me. We need to gather and work together in reforming the United States as it once was. We have room for some of you now and will return for the rest of you later.

Laura has placed some forms on the table. Those of you who wish to accept this offer please fill them out and soon a Government Representative will arrive here to work with you on resettlement."

The next day the President and Laura are taken to the other shelters. He gives the same speech to each group.

Will wonders if this was to be the end of the Phoenix Clan. The next few days would tell.

A NEW DAY ARRIVES
CHAPTER TWELVE

"Phoenix this is Ernest."

"Go ahead Ernest."

"How is the weather there?"

"Cold but clear."

"Then we are headed your way. ETA 1100hrs your time tomorrow."

"We will be ready for you how many passengers will you have?"

"Approximately eight-hundred, but don't worry about feeding them. They will be fed on the planes. We will service and immediately takeoff for Savanna."

"Roger, we will be ready for your arrival, out."

Frank and Laura spend the last evening at Shelter Two. They to convince Will to move to Savannah and encourage the others to do likewise.

"The others are free to do as they please. As I told you this is a free society and no one tells another what to do. When help is needed we ask for it. - My blood family met last night and discussed moving. In a secret ballot, every vote read stay here. You may need us to be here in the long run. We will maintain the airport in case it is ever again needed."

"Well if I can not convince you to go, is there anything I

can do for you."

"We are in bad need of a helicopter that uses regular gas. Incidentally we have stored seeds of many kind and as you saw are prepared to restock the streams with fish. Our chicken population will be sufficient to furnish meat and eggs for everyone here soon. The cattle brought to us from Hawaii will become a herd in a few years and we have fruit trees within the shelter ready for transplant outside. Perhaps we can in the years to come establish a trade partnership with those in Savannah."

"I will check on the helicopter. We also have the expertise to restore an electrical generating plant in this area if that would help."

"Thanks anyway but my sons are already working on that and also a city water distribution system to the airport. Our farmers are set to plant cotton and the boys are working on repairing the cloth factory in Cedartown. We'll have local telephone service restored by summer. If enough people stay here, we have plans to build a new town near the airport and restore a church and the park in Cave Spring."

"Well your clan has certainly proven it can perform miracles. I will not pressure anyone else to go. You are right this area is important to the resurrection of our nation and your people seem to have it worked out."

"I will know our strength tomorrow when we see how many are leaving with you."

Right on time the C-141s land at the Phoenix Clan Airport and after a fast turnaround prepare to leave for Savannah. Martha and a twenty-two others say goodbye and board the

Command Center aircraft. Ernest presents Will with a Hawaiian Lei and a crate of fresh pineapples. Before he boards his craft he tells Will.

"Thank everyone for us and you will be hearing from me. I think this would be the ideal place to retire."

They shake hands and Ernest goes to board his aircraft.

The Airborne Command aircraft has been serviced and the President will use it to return to Savannah. Will wishes him and Laura well and a safe flight. At the top of the loading ramp Frank turns.

"I will not forsake our Phoenix Clan. You will hear from me Will Ferguson Phoenix."

With the Presidents aircraft leading the way all the aircraft taxi to the runway and takeoff. Everyone on the ground stares at the ski until the aircraft are just dots and then nothing.

Kelly seems to say what is on everyone's mind.

"I wonder when we will see them again. Will - Howard's family, Melvin's family, Hank's family and mine have decided to live here at the airport and help build the town you talked about."

"That's good I will see to it each family receives the deed to five-hundred acres in the near the airport."

Two mornings later, aircraft can be heard in a distance. Kelly and others hustle to their positions. They call Shelter one and notify Will who gathers his sons and heads for the airport. When they arrive they find five 141s and a medium sized civilian cargo aircraft on the tarmac. Ernest is near the first aircraft in line. Will greets him.

"Its good to see you again so soon. What's going on?"

"The fuel trucks we left here were empty so we are going to return them to Savannah and we brought others to replace them. This way fuel will be available here if the need arises."

"That's great we appreciate it. Who is in the civilian aircraft?

"Its not who but what that's important. Come and let me show you."

Two small civilian helicopters are being offloaded from the plane as they approach..

"These and this aircraft are a present from George."

"What can I say. With the choppers we can scout a larger area for supplies and the aircraft can be used to establish trade with Central and South America. I must write A letter to thank the President."

"Can you use a pilot? I have retired from the Air Force."

Ernest hesitates as his voice breaks.

"I lost my wife and sons in the war and now the Phoenix Clan is the only family I have."

"I am sorry about your wife and children. -- You were a family member here from the time you asked me to call you Ernest."

Will extends his hand to Earnest and says what he never heard when he returned home from Viet Nam so many years ago.

"WELCOME HOME."

"Thanks Will that means a lot to me."

"The electronic technicians have connected Savanna to satellites and they now have the capability of communicating with the surviving world. Frank has re-established relations with most countries that still exist and he dreams of rebuilding Washington. He says with what he saw here, he is convinced it can be done."

Laughing Will comments.

"It might be hard to gather volunteers to do that."

"Oh, his Shadow Government already has the new American money coming off the presses. Most of Savannah's building are intact and he is setting up a temporary national government there."

"I guess politicians will always be politicians. I wonder if it has come to him yet that his two terms in office have passed?"

"He wants a Senator and Representative from here for the New Legislative part of the government. - I am sure the first order of business before them will be to extend his term.

The worst problem so far has been burying the half-million or so corpses in the area.

"It took us weeks just to clear the local area here. At least there are no longer flies or other insects to cause diseases to spread from the bodies. We had no choice but to bury them in mass graves which we marked as victims of America's Final War."

Colonel Yeager approaches them.

"We are ready and we had best be going before we are snowed in."

Will asks Colonel Yeager.

"Does that new government have weather forecasting equipment. We could sure use some if it is available."

"I'll check and let you know. So long for now."

He boards his aircraft and is ready to depart. But the clan's aircraft has the way blocked.

Ernest tells Will.

"Come on lets move our aircraft out of their way."

With Will in the co-pilot seat Ernest taxies the bird onto the runway. He then calls Kelly and asks permission to takeoff.

Will looks at Ernest, but does not say a word as the aircraft rolls down the runway and leaves the slippery bonds of earth.

"I thought you might like to check out our new bird and also get a birds eye view of the accomplishments of the Phoenix Clan."

Will sits back and enjoys a freedom of worry that he had not known in a long time. He somehow wished they never had to land, but knew each moment of enjoyment up here meant the burning of precious jet fuel. - He reluctantly looks at Earnest.

"We had best go down now and preserve our fuel."

After landing they went and talked to Kelly. Kelly had talked to Colonel Yeager and had learned their will be other flights to and from the Phoenix Airport. Kelly states to Will.

"Well that was a surprise. I wonder how often that will happen."

To which Will answers.

"There will be occasional flights but I doubt if we will ever see that many aircraft here again at one time. I'm glad they came. We how have a capability we didn't have before. -- Lets put the helicopters inside for now. -- When the weather is better we will recon the Atlanta area and see if there is anything left there."

The weather once more becomes bad and again no one is able to leave the shelters. This allows the residents time to discuss what they will do with the rest of their lives. Plans are made to re-establish different types of businesses. Life would never be as before the war but in many ways it was better for those who had survived. They were now a close knit family who had learned to work together for the good of all.

By late March, most of the ice and snow was gone and the ladies begin making plans for the Easter get together.

Mary Ann in almost a dreaming fashion.

"It would be nice if we had eggs for an old fashion Easter egg hunt."

To which Carmon responds.

"Well lets made some we have plenty of colored paper and glue in the craft supplies."

They set about doing just that.

One day while watching the news on a Mexican television station the following is heard. "The Mexican Government is once again fully in place. Millions have survived by temporally moving to the South. Many have returned to their homes in the Northern part of the country. President Fernandez has declared Mexico is reclaiming the territory taken from it by the United States in 1848. This includes West Texas, Southern New Mexico, Southern Arizona and Southern California.."

Will thought out loud.

"I wonder if Frank will try to prevent this and mankind will once again be at war? God knows I hope not."

On Easter morning, everyone comes out of the shelter. Most have not been outside since before Christmas. It is a beautiful day with no wind. The sun is shining and it is sixty degrees. They walk around while waiting for the vehicles to be made ready. Suddenly Teresa yells.

"Will come and look at this."

Will and others rush over wondering what she has found to get her so excited.

"Look a seedling things are beginning to grow again."

Linda looks around.

"Look at the hillside it is beginning to turn green with new growth."

"Billy lead us in prayer. Man had scorched the earth and God is about to replenish it."

Will and Teresa are bending over looking at the seedling when Teresa's body stiffens and she falls back into Will's arms. As he holds her he also lays back. Teresa calls for him with a weak voice.

"Will."

"I know darling. don't be afraid I'm coming with you."

As their spirits float free of their bodies they look down and see their family all huddled around the bodies. A passive light appears in the distance and the voice of God is heard.

"Well done my children. Now come home."

Arm in arm their spirits float toward the light.

THE NEW BEGINNING

YOU CAN SURVIVE
IF YOU ARE PROPERLY PREPARED

The future will sooner or later surely bring the war described within this book. It is a fact that terrorist attacks have become a way of life with many countries of the world. The United States has also been attacked many time over the last eleven years. I thought September 11, would open everyone's eyes and it did for most, at least for a short while. The majority of the terrorist performing these attacks belong to the organizations heretofore mentioned. Their goal is to take one country at a time and eventually take over the world.

Before this happens, Israel and NATO will try to destroy them. I hope they succeed, before the terrorist organizations destroy the United States.

===

The design of the shelter used in this book is sound. Architectural drawings and the survival manual will soon be available. Send all inquires to.

> McElwee & Company
> P. O. Box 465
> Cave Spring, Georgia
> 30124

VIET NAM 1966-67

Viet Nam was Johnson's hell on earth for those of us that were there. The people of the United States, our military and the world were never told why we were involved.

This book covers some of the things that happened to this author and gives information which had it been made public might have changed the opinion of many concerning the war and the military that fought it.

Most people are still as confused about this war as the character studying the road signs.

VIET NAM 1966-67

"WILL I LIVE THROUGH THIS?" This thought is bound to enter the minds of all who go to war. Movies make it out to be a thrilling adventure. Sherman originally said it and it has been repeated many times. "War is hell." I add, "Here on earth." It is neither a romantic nor macho adventure. I was fully aware of this when the Air Force ordered me to Tan Son Nhut.

My tour in Viet Nam began December 24, 1966. President Johnson had just ordered the huge buildup of US troops there. I had assumed upon landing the Air Force would take care of my need of sleeping quarters and food.. Boy was I wrong. Several hundred of us arrived together and were directed into a briefing area. Where we were told, "The army Chow Hall will feed E-4's and below. You NCOs are on your on. Go find your outfit and report in. -- By the way, welcome to Johnson's Hell."

Several of us found the Chief of Maintenances Offices and reported to the Maintenance Superintendent. As I entered, he looked up and surprised me, by calling me by name and pronouncing it correctly. (note: few people do)

"How do you know me?"

"Years ago, I had five airmen working under me. I owned a bitch dog and when she littered with five puppies I named them after my airmen. I still have McElwee."

Well at least my tour was starting with a laugh.

"Which section do you want to work in?"

"I went to school on the RF-4 before I came over so I guess with these."

"You can have the T-39 Section if you want it."

"No thanks I'll stick with the RF-4s."

I believe certain things happen to us for reasons we sometimes don't understand. They are just meant to be. Even as I turned down the T-39s, I was asking myself why I did so. I could only think God must want me with the RF-4s.

The NCO behind me spoke up, "I've worked 39s before, can I have um?" This individual was soon making regular flights to and from the states and I reported to the 12th TAC to work with RF-4s. These birds only flew at night. I was glad of this as most attacks on the base occurred at night and I preferred being awake and dressed when we were hit.

Chief ------- Told me where there was a newly built empty barracks and a storeroom full of bunks. Two others and I were the first to move in there. No lockers were available, so we lived out of our luggage. Within two days the barracks was filled to capacity with double bunks so close together it looked like one long bunk bed from one end of the room to the other. The only way to get in and out of your bed was to crawl over the foot rail and there was still no lockers.

At first glance, the base appeared similar to ones stateside. Boy did that change in a hurry. Since we were to work at night, Sergeant McDonald, Sergeant Beamer and I decided to check out Saigon. After all it looked peaceful enough. We took a taxi downtown to the Street of Flowers. This street had been made famous in the novel, "The Ugly American."

We had just stepped from the cab onto the sidewalk and were about to explore the sights when gunshots rang out. We turned and saw a man with half his head blown off laying on the sidewalk just behind us. Two White Mice (Vietnamese Police) had fired the shots. They came running over. One of them reached into the man's pocket, pulled out a hand grenade, looked up at us and smiling said, "Viet Cong." So much for our relaxed manner. We immediately entered the Saigon Bar, which was full of Americans. We also learned that this bar was often targeted by the communist. Several American's had died there during these attacks.

The next day I got lucky. I met the NCO in charge of assigning personnel to the NCOBQ's in downtown Saigon. He had one empty space and I got it. This turned out to be on the eighth floor of the Halverson Hotel. The elevator didn't work, but believe me, I didn't mind that. Although it had been a hotel, it was now a NCO Barracks for Air Force personnel. I had a roommate and the only furniture was GI bunks.

Each evening, several of us were picked up and taken to the base in a truck with chicken wire wrapped around it to prevent grenades from being pitched in from the sides. Our First Shirt was a Master Sergeant Smith who had retired before the war started and had volunteered to return to active duty. Each evening he sat on the tailgate with his weapon at ready.

One evening, a boy that couldn't have been over ten years old ran from an alley, as we passed it. The boy tossed a grenade toward the back of the truck. Smitty swung the butt of his rifle and batted the grenade away as if it was a baseball. It exploded in the street behind us. Before this happened, we had kidded Sgt. Smith about riding shotgun for us. After this incident, we praised him for his vigilance and good reflexes. No doubt, everyone in that truck would have been sent home in body bags if he had missed and the grenade had entered the truck. It worried me that so young a boy could hate us enough to try and kill us.

Once a week an Army Colonel briefed us and I asked him about this. His answer was bone chilling.

"The Communist keep the civilian populace under a cloud of fear. More than likely they had kidnapped the boys family and told him they would all be killed if he did not throw that grenade. Since he failed, he was probably shot as an example to others."

The truck came at the same time every evening and we waited in the same area, leaning against a wall outside the hotel. One day when we arrived there was a five gallon bucket by the wall and I naively started to sit on it while waiting for the truck. God was surely watching over us that evening, because the truck came early. We were less than a half block away when the bomb under the bucket exploded. The wall was destroyed and debris peppered the truck as we drove away. Once again death was narrowly escaped. After that as ranking NCO, I was very careful as to where we waited for the truck. I changed our pickup point often.

We had no weapons to defend ourselves if attacked The military Commander, General W---------- had decided that Air Force personnel other than the Air Police would not be armed. The Army was responsible for out security. I don't know to this day where Smitty got his M-16.

I had been there only two days when the enemy sent a suicide squad onto the base. The base perimeter was over a mile from the aircraft parking areas. A binjo ditch (sewage) ran behind the CIA's aircraft, (C-47s). Around 0400hrs black suited Vietnamese came out of this ditch. They had dug a tunnel which led from outside the base into this ditch. The tunnel went under two runways of what was then the busiest airport in the world.

My cousin, David Ferguson was the NCO in charge of the crews responsible for maintaining the Gooney Birds (A. F. name for C-47s). When he saw the communist coming from the ditch, he ordered his men to lay on the ground and play dead. The enemy carried no firearms only satchel charges on their backs. One of the Vietnamese, stepped on David's head and spun around grinding his face into the gravel. He then threw his satchel charge into the open door of one of the aircraft destroying it.

An Air Policeman was in a bunker across the taxiway from me. He was positioned to protect the 16th TAC Squadron. This young man attempted to fire his weapon as a black suited communist soldier ran toward him. For some reason that I will never understand, he was armed with a shotgun. The gun jammed and the enemy threw his satchel into the bunker killing this American Soldier. Finely, other Air Police arrived with a machinegun firing from the back of a jeep and handled the situation.

During this, one of the strangest things I have ever witnessed occurred, a South Vietnamese soldier came from a nearby underground bunker, walked up behind the jeep and calmly filled his cup from a coffee container. Considering the stress he was under, I am sure if the airman on the machinegun had noticed the Vietnamese behind him he would have shot him.

The next morning, T/Sgt Ferguson went to General W----------'s office and demanded that the Air Force be allowed weapons to defend their self. If he and his troops had been armed, they could have stopped the enemy before they killed Americans and destroyed the C-47.

That evening, I was given the extra title of Night Security Officer of the 12th TAC and a weapon was made available to me. David also received one.

In early October, the base was attacked by a large enemy force. The Army sent out everyone available to defend the base. Improperly trained clerks and supply personnel who shot at everything that moved were included. Several Americans were among those hit by friendly fire that night. The next day General W------------ informed the Army Commander that from then on the Air Force would defend the base. He then changed the name of the Air Police to Security Police.

Since entering the Air Force I had always been in charge of something. In Basic Training, I was a Squad Leader and shortly after arriving at my first assignment from basic I was put in charge of a crew of aircraft mechanics. This continued until I arrived in Viet Nam. When I reported to the 12th TAC, I was happy to find that many outranked me and I was assigned as Crew Chief of only one RF-4. Unfortunately this was to soon change. My new outfit was an Air National Guard Squadron and only seven assigned with them were regular Air Force, one five level Staff Sergeant, five Airmen Second Class and I (At the time a seven level Staff Sergeant).

One evening when reporting for duty, I found only the regulars were there. I immediately called Maintenance Control and asked where the others were. They didn't seem to know what I was talking about. I was put on hold for about five minutes, then a Colonel C----- came on the line.

"How many men do you have?"

"There are seven of us."

"Is this Sgt. McElwee?"

"Yes."

"The mission has not changed. Handle it Mc."

He then hung up the telephone. What must be done was evident. I called the men into formation.

"You've been talking about what you could do if you were allowed to, now you're going to show everyone." (Note: prior to this airmen below the rank of E-5 were only allowed to refuel and perform other minor duties on the 12th's aircraft.)

I then looked at the Staff Sergeant.

"You are as of this moment Assistant Flight Chief. Assign each airman as Crew Chief of two aircraft and I want their names on their planes before the first mission. You have about an hour before our first flight. I want every aircraft preflighted and ready for flight fifteen minutes before the first pilot arrives. You move from aircraft to aircraft assisting as necessary. I'll be around to release the forms and answer questions."

These airmen came through like the professionals they were. Not only that night, but for the next three months. I became the Flight Chief and was so busy I never noticed that no orders were ever cut assigning me as such. When I returned stateside and received a copy of my Performance Report during this period I was shocked. The report had me listed as a Crew Chief. It started off.

"Sgt. McElwee has at times been given the responsibility of supervision over more than just his aircraft, which he does with willingness and great enthusiasm."

Since I an E-5, had performed in a E-9 position and the airmen under me had set new RF-4 in commission records during our three months under the responsibility I can only assume the powers to be were embarrassed to admit what had been accomplished by so few lower ranking airmen.

After changing an engine on one of the aircraft, it was necessary to tow it to the Run Up Pad, operate the engine through all throttle settings and make adjustments as necessary. The Run Up Pad was near the perimeter of the base so I wasted no time in the testing. We had just started back when I noticed a Metro (truck) bearing down on us. His lights were off and he was coming fast. As he pulled near us, I stopped and jumped from the Coleman (tow vehicle).

"What's wrong?"

"Look behind you."

The area was full of enemy soldiers and they were closing on us fast. It's a wonder that I didn't pull the nose gear from the RF-4 as I jumped back into the Coleman and pressed the accelerator to the floor.

As we moved away, Puff The Magic Dragon (note: this was what we called a C-47 gunship) passed over us with his 50mm Gatling Guns blasting away. Puff was followed by a helicopter gunship also firing on the enemy.

Before this I had little respect for Technical Sergeant --------

because of his attitude while doing his job. There is no doubt, he saved the airman's and my life that night at the risk of his own. From then on, I had great respect for him.

After parking the aircraft, I took my position with the M-16 at ready. The Security Policeman next to me in a sandbag bunker looked over at me.

"What do we do Sgt."

I had wondered what I would do if I was ever put in this position now I was about to find out.

"The best we can son."

The enemy was about a quarter mile from us and all hell was breaking loose when a voice came over the radio. It was a wounded Security Policeman. It was obvious, he was a very young man.

"They killed my dog uh, uh, I'm hurt bad."

Even as he was dying this airman was worried about his dog. The body count of the enemy from that night was in the hundreds, but to me this was not enough to atone for that one young American who died performing his duty.

About six months into my tour, a SSgt. NCO Dining Hall opened on base. It was a relatively small building surrounded by the highest double chain link fence I have ever seen. One day I decided to eat there before going on duty. The entrance was guarded by a Vietnamese soldier and you had to weave your way through barriers to enter. One of the guys, had a radio and when we sat down he tuned it to Hanoi Radio. We often listened to Hanna on this station because she played the latest music from back home. She also preached Communist propaganda in English and just as we began to eat she announced.

"Our glorious Army has destroyed the new American Air Force NCO Dining Hall on Tan SON Nhut Air Base near Saigon."

I jumped up and ran outside. Against the wall where we were sitting was a large paper bag. I yelled at the guard to call EOD (bomb squad), then rushed inside and ordered everyone to evacuate the building. The bag contained a powerful bomb. By the time, EOD disarmed the bomb its timer had less than five minutes remaining. Everyone then went back inside and finished their dinner. Once again God had intervened to save many lives. If we had not turned on the radio, or if Hanna had taken ten more minutes before making her announcement I would not be here to write this.

In the mornings, I was usually dropped off on the corner a block from the hotel. Each day, I walked pass an Elementary School. At first when I passed the children would run away from the fence and just stare. They were afraid of me. I always smiled and waved at them. I did not realize at the time that the Communist kept the general populace in line by killing women and children. In time, the children came to the fence smiling and jabbering away. It was clear they no longer saw me as dangerous.

One morning as I passed the school, I witnessed the worst sight imaginable. The school had been mortared and body parts of what had been happy children were scattered about the schoolyard. I will go to my grave wondering if these children were slaughtered because of me befriending them.

When I reached my room, I automatically turned on the radio and fell unto my bunk. Hanoi Jane Fonda was screaming.

"Last night Americans bombed a house and killed a mother and her child. American baby killers did this."

I grabbed the radio, pulled it from the wall and started to throw it out the window. Luckily I caught myself in time. The street below was full of people and had I thrown the radio from eight stories up someone could have been killed. This was during the time when President Johnson allowed only unarmed reconnaissance flights over Hanoi. The 12th (my aircraft) and the 16th flew these missions. The commies fired ground to air rockets at our aircraft. We never had an aircraft hit by one of them.

Ask yourself, if I fire a rocket into the air and it hits nothing, what will happen to that rocket? The same thing happened to the commie rockets, they fell back to earth upon their own people. This Fonda creature then blamed the Americans and labeled us baby killers. Where was she when the school was mortared? The answer is easy. She was in the company of the monsters that ordered the killing of these innocent children.

I was lucky enough to find and purchase a small television set. Each evening I watched the evening news from the states. (note: we received the news over the Armed Forces Network a day later than people in the states.) One day W----- C------- announced.

"Today the Halverson Hotel an Air Force NCOBQ was destroyed by enemy mortars."

The screen then showed what appeared to be the hotel with flames coming from its windows. Some reported had doctored a video. It looked as though the hotel was being gutted by fire.

The hotel was not air-conditioned so everyone left their doors open allowing air to circulate. The Sgt across from the hall from me was an Air Force Times Reporter, I yelled out

"Hey are you watching this?

His response shocked me.

"Are you watching state side news/"

"Yes."

"Don't you know civilian reporters get paid according to how much of their material is used. Few actually go out in the battle zones for their stories. Most of them get their material from drunk soldiers in the Saigon Bar."

"But I'm watching a video of this building burning."

"Camera and lab tricks are common. If you want to hear tomorrow's news go down to the bar and just listen."

"But what about the video with the stories?"

"Watch them closely as some of them are from real reporters during the Korean War or earlier. Look at the uniforms and equipment."

He also called the names of reporters that are easily recognized.

"Go down to the bar this evening an look around. You will see reporters that you recognize. --- ----------, --- -------, etc"

After this, I never watched state side news. I did however determine some reporters were misrepresenting the war for their own financial gain.

An event had taken place a few days earlier that could have made the hotel burning report true if not for an alert Vietnamese guard. Sgt ------- Also lived in the room across the hall from me. Looking down and across the street from his room, the view was a cemetery. One day, he ran into my room.

"They are setting up a mortar in the cemetery."

I jumped up from the bed.

"Come on."

The fifth floor of the hotel had an outside walkway which circled the building and a South Vietnamese guard was on duty. We ran down the stairs to warn him. He was sitting in a chair with his head down as if asleep. Hearing us coming, he motioned us back.

"I see. -- Stay back."

The mortar was set up and shells were being unloaded from a taxi when, he sprang into action. He sat upright, aimed and fired his weapon. Two of the enemy were killed, but the taxi driver got away.

I could not help but wonder, did an American or ally reporter know about this impending attack and by mistake release the story before it happened showing it as a successful attack on Americans. The attempt was sure close to what I had seen on American television supposedly the real thing.

One night in mid December, I looked down the ramp to see the most Zebras (high ranking NCOs) I had ever seen in one group on the flightline. There was a Chief Master Sergeant, two Senior Master Sergeants, six or so Master Sergeants, and many Tech and Staff Sergeants. Our relief had finely arrived. The Chief came over to me.

"Sgt McElwee we are your replacements."

I arrived back in the states Dec 24, 1977 aboard a C-141 which landed at Kelly Air Force Base in San Antonio, Texas. My brother-in-Law Johnny and his wife Linda met me and took me to their house. From there I called and reserved a first class ticket on a commercial aircraft heading to Atlanta. I then called my wife and gave her my estimated time of arrival.

I had heard about the mistreatment American military men and women were receiving upon returning home but really didn't expect to encounter any. I was dressed in my class A uniform and had paid to fly in the first class section. The stewardesses totally ignored me until just before we landed. One finely looked my way and without smiling.

"Oh; do you want anything?"

My family was waiting when I deplaned and at that point nothing else mattered. I had survived Johnson's Hell and had returned to the ones I loved. Even today I can't look at the names on the Viet Nam Memorial Wall. I don't want to know how many members of the 12th TAC, who didn't make it to duty that evening back in Viet Nam, are listed there.

The patriots who answered their countries call to arms did not go to this far off land to serve their country and then return to be treated as criminals, to be called horrible things and be spit upon.

They went because their government called upon them to do so. No one ever explained to them or anyone else why they were there. Your government and the news media knew, but they didn't bother to tell anyone. Why I can not imagine. I believe, the news media did not, because the longer the war lasted, the bigger the protest thus the bigger the story.

France controlled Viet Nam as a colony from 1883 until 1954, except for during WW-II. The Vietnamese had always resisted French rule and in 1946 the Viet Minh began a revolution against it. In 1954, the battle of Dien Bien Phu ended French control. In 1955, with The United States mediating, the two main factions that had defeated the French agreed to form two independent nations with the Communist to the north and the Republic of South Viet Nam to the south.

The United States also became involved in transporting to the south those who did not wish to live under Communist rule. Over one million people were flown south from Hanoi.

The following is a quote from the Encyclopedia Americana, 1961 edition.

"The United States gave the new Southern Regime substantial financial and technical aid. In 1955, the United States and the Republic of South Viet Nam signed a treaty. This treaty guaranteed American assistance should South Viet Nam ever be attacked."

<u>This treaty was the reason so many fought and died there and strict control from the White House over the United States military was the reason we did not win the war.</u>